Love Is Blind

Vanessa Sarlton

Published by Trellis Publishing, 2021.

This is a work of fiction. Similarities to real people, places, or events are entirely coincidental.

LOVE IS BLIND

First edition. June 30, 2021.

Copyright © 2021 Vanessa Sarlton.

ISBN: 979-8224170951

Written by Vanessa Sarlton.

LOVE IS BLIND

A MAIL ORDER BRIDE ROMANCE
VANESSA SARLTON

Chapter One

Life has never been easy for Phoebe Walston. And, it wasn't about to get easier.

She paced around her room, gathering dresses and other belongings. They went flying into her worn leather suitcase.

"Oh, dear! You mustn't treat your dresses like this! They'll be ruined." Milly, her childhood best friend rushed forward to salvage what she could. With a practiced hand, she folded them into neat little squares before placing them back into the suitcase. "Really, Feebs, I understand why you're in such a rush to run away with your paw being full as a tick all the time but you can't just go off all willy-nilly without any sort of direction. What'll you do?"

"I reckon I'll figure out a way." Phoebe continued to rummage through her wardrobe. "I hear the factories up north take in female workers. Think they'd take a biddy like me?" Phoebe paused beside her window. Through the glass she watched her mother stumbling through the streets. Her bodice had been torn down the middle, exposing her milky-white chest. Her bonnet was nowhere to be seen. A couple of men standing at the local saloon hollered at her knowing full well that she was one of the town's painted women.

Her mother turned and offered them a toothless smile. As she lifted her skirts, she walked over to them, her eyes dull and glazed over.

Phoebe couldn't bear to watch her any longer.

"What are you going to do, hun?" Milly whispered.

"Light a shuck and get the hell out of here." Phoebe slumped onto her bed, head in her hands. "But, I'm awfully scared, Milly."

"This might horse-feathered idea but it might just be crazy enough to work." As she spoke, she reached into her bag and retrieved the Sunday paper.

"What's that?"

"*The Yorker.*" She explained. "My maw was having tea with a couple of her friends and I overheard them talking about this..." She trailed off as she flipped through the pages trying to find the right one. "Ah, here it is."

Phoebe peered over her shoulder, head cocked. "What the devil is this?" All she could see was a page full of photographs. She snatched the paper and squinted at the blurry images. "Who in tarnation are these men?"

"They're men looking for wives."

"*Wives?*" Phoebe repeated. "You're pulling my leg."

Milly shook her head causing her tight curls to bounce against her shoulders. "I swear on my soul! They put out ads on the paper looking for a wife."

"Why on Earth would they do such a thing?"

"You see, most of 'em live in the West where there ain't nothin' but rattlesnakes and redskins." Milly tightened her tone to a thick twang as she hooked her fingers into the waistline of her bodice, impersonating the stance of a cowboy. "Them gunslingers need ladies too, I reckon."

"You want me to get hitched to a gunslinger?" Phoebe raised her eyebrows in surprise. "Have you lost your mind?"

"Better than this load of bull crap you have to deal with every day. I've heard great things about the West – land of liberation. Women can do as they please and if someone gets in your way you just put plum between his eyes. *Bang! Bang!*" She held out two fingers and cocked them, pretending to fire a gun. "Think about it, Feebs. Heck, if I wasn't already engaged, I'd get on a train and follow you out there. Meet me a handsome cowboy and ride into the sunset with him."

Phoebe rolled her eyes. Milly had always been a dreamer. She romanticized the idea of marriage, painting it into some wonderful landscape of happiness but Phoebe was no stranger to the harsh reality. People got married because that was just something they did. A girl needed a man to survive in this world and that was just how things were. She was no different.

So, with a sigh, she scanned her options. Halfway down the page, she stopped. The picture was significantly better than all the others, brighter in contrast and taken at a better angle, highlighting the man's strong jawline. She couldn't be quite sure she sensed a pair of dark steel-colored eyes. Paired with a clean-shaven look this man was definitely a cut above the rest.

"Clayton Swift..." She whispered aloud. "I like the sound of that."

"Is that your boy?" Milly giggled. "He's a handsome devil."

"I haven't made up my mind yet!"

"You have this look in your eyes, Feebs. I'd recognize it anywhere. You've already fallen head over heels in love with this man."

"Oh, put a cork in it, will you?"

Milly giggled once more. "Are you going to answer his ad?"

Phoebe ignored her friend as she read the description underneath his photograph.

Clayton Swift is willing to provide a healthy God-fearing with a steady income and a nice place to live. Situated in Wyoming, Swift would prefer a woman who has experience with housekeeping and is capable of running an Inn. Compensation will be provided. Additionally, his future wife must be willing to care and tend for his little boy, Boone. If interested, please send a telegram to...

Phoebe didn't bother to read the rest. "He's widowed."

"So?" Milly cracked the window. "It's hotter than hell today, ain't it?"

"It's always been stuffy in here." Phoebe pointed out.

"I don't know how you stand it. This place is about ready to roast a couple of hens."

"Milly, what do you reckon I should do?" Unable to stay still, she got up and paced around her room. "I can't just up and marry a fellow I haven't met, can I?"

Crash!

Phoebe flinched.

Her father was at it again. "Not even noon yet and he's already taking swigs at the bottle." She cursed under her breath. "That's it. Anything's better than *this*." She turned toward Milly, features pinched with her determination. "When's the next train to Wyoming. I'm getting the hell out of here!"

Crash!

Chapter 2

Maybe riding to Wyoming all by herself wasn't the best thing for Phoebe to do. As she endured the bumpy ride across the country, she sat as stiff as a rod, holding onto her bag so tightly that she had lost all feeling in her fingers.

Through her window, she admired the Western landscape decorated with nothing but corn stalks and wide-open spaces. Occasionally, she'd spot a herd of cattle but they were few and far between.

"Think the redskins will show up?" A deep, gruff voice broke the silence that had settled inside the cab. "They hijacked a train only last week. You know, I wouldn't mind letting a couple of 'em hang." Phoebe turned slightly in her seat and watched the man take out his pistol and start polishing it. She tightened her grip on her bag. It wasn't much but at least it would buy her a few good hits in case any of these low-life men decided to try anything with her.

She had noticed them eyeballing her like she was some sort of heifer or something. Just the thought made her sick to her stomach. She ground her teeth together, praying that she was almost there.

"I'd like to see those varmint step foot on my property. They'd be dead faster than a fish in a barrel."

***

Eventually, Phoebe reached her destination. She gathered her belongings, took a deep breath, and stepped onto the platform. There, the sun blazed overhead, reflecting off the sandy terrain, making it's light even brighter. Phoebe squinted, raising her hand to her brow.

She couldn't see a darned thing.

"Paw, where is she?"

"She'll be here any second, I reckon."

"Is she nice, paw?"

"Boy, quit your yammering. She'll get here when she gets here."

It took a moment for Phoebe's vision to adjust to the sunlight but once it did, she realized she was standing right in front of Clayton Swift although, he had yet to notice her.

She stood there, struck by his devilishly good looks. His photograph in the paper really did him no justice at all. Broad shoulders. Tall as a spruce tree. Tanned like a good ol' piece of toffee. And those eyes. The color of a brand spanking new Winchester.

What this man really going to become her husband? Sure, he might be attractive but he could be as crooked as a snake for all she knew. This could very well be the biggest mistake of her life. Still, she had made her decision and planned to stick with it.

"Excuse me." She cleared her throat, suddenly feeling like a frog had lodged itself in her windpipes. Her lips were impossibly dry and when she tried to moisten them her tongue turned into a rock.

"Yes?" Clayton turned, tipping his hat in her direction. "May I help you, Ma'am?"

"I'm Phoebe Walton. I answered your ad in the paper." For some reason, her cheeks reddened as she spoke. The circumstances around their relationship were certainly... strange. In a way, she felt like an easy woman for doing this. Normal girls found a nice boy in town, courted them, and then tied the knot. But Phoebe had always been a little different.

"Ah, it's a pleasure." He smiled, showing off a rather nice set of teeth.

It awakened a swarm of butterflies inside Phoebe's stomach. Her heart started to pound, growing louder and louder with each passing minute. Beads of sweat formed at the back of her neck.

Why was she feeling this way? It must be the heat, she told herself.

"Is it her?" The little boy standing beside Clayton asked.

It was then that Phoebe noticed the whiteness of his eyes. His irises were void of color with a milky film running across the entire socket.

"This here is my son, Boone."

Phoebe smiled at the little boy even though it was quite obvious that he was blind. "It's so nice to finally meet you, Boone." She bent over, took his hand, and squeezed it gently. "I hope you don't mind me joining the family."

"Not at all!" He exclaimed, turning his head in her direction. "We've been awfully excited to meet you, ma'am. It gets lonely just the two of us."

Clayton ran his fingers through his son's thick hair. "He's a scalawag of a boy but he's going to turn out into a fine young man one of these days. But I can't raise him on my own. He needs some feminine guidance if you 'stand what I mean."

"I'll certainly do my best."

"Here, let me take your bags." Clayton offered as he picked up her luggage with utter ease.

"Oh, you don't have to. I've carried them up until this point."

"Pshaw, 'taint no trouble 'tall." Again, he smiled at her and again her heart seemed to rocket out of her chest. She blushed, looking away. No man had ever made her feel this way before. Every inch of her skin felt like hot embers on a fire. "Come, our new home is this aways."

Our new home, Phoebe repeated in her head. Maybe, just maybe, this was the fresh start she had always prayed for.

"I'll show you the way!" The little boy exclaimed as he took her hand.

"But..." She started.

Clayton shook his head, a knowing smile on his head. "You'll see."

Click. Click. Click.

"What's he doing?" She cocked her head, confused.

"Honestly, I don't quite know myself. I just know it works." Clayton shrugged his shoulders. "Lets him get around without bumping into everything. It's strange, let me tell you, but it's sorta nice, ain't it?"

Phoebe listened to the little boy as he clicked his tongue against the roof of his mouth. Somehow, the sound helped him navigate.

With a confident stride, Boone guided his soon-to-be step-mother into town.

Chapter 3

The following Saturday night.

Phoebe had taken the week to settle into her new home. For the most part, she was enjoying her time in Wyoming. Clayton was incredibly kind to her. Things were still a bit stiff and awkward between the two of them but she could see herself warming up to him soon, especially since they were already husband and wife.

"Boone, mind grabbing the bed linen for me? They're in the washroom."

"Yes, Ma'am."

As Phoebe tidied one of the guest room she could hear Boone's clicking. It was still strange to witness a blind boy walking around, unperturbed and confident, but she was quickly getting used to the sight.

Bang!

"Oh, stop bellerin' like a hog, Eustice. We've heard enough of your complaining. If you don't like my prices, get the hell out or the next time this plum is going between your eyes, got that?"

"You cain't shoot center, Randal. Couldn't shoot me if you had the barrel to my forehead." The drunken man snickers, staggering forward, holding his belly with laughter.

"What's going on?" Boone appeared with the sheets bundled into his arms.

"Nothing." Phoebe shook her head. "It's nothing."

Life in the West was rough. Men shot at each other just for giving one another a dirty stare. People were constantly yelling. Booze ran like water through the veins of these cowboys. She wasn't particularly fond of their manners, neither. Luckily, Clayton seemed to be one of the few that knew how to keep his wits about him.

"There." Phoebe flattened out a couple of wrinkles and fluffed up the pillows. "I reckon that good enough for the Queen."

Boone ran his hand along the edge of the bed. "Phoebe, are you going to stay for a long time?"

"A very long time, don't you worry." She ruffled up his hair and smiled. "I promised to take good care of you and your paw and that's exactly what I intend to do, or so help me God."

"Promise?"

"Promise."

***

That night, everything changed. Phoebe couldn't find Clayton anywhere.

"Boone, do you know where your paw up and went off to? I can't find hide nor tail of that man." Phoebe stood in the doorway, hand on her hip. "He should have been home by now."

Boone frowned. "Um..."

She narrowed her eyes in his direction. Clearly, he knew something and he was trying to hide it from her.

"Boone..." She whispered, sitting down beside me. "You can tell me."

"He's at the saloon. It's right next door. Every Saturday he sits up with his friends. Usually caterwauling by the end of the night. Comes home fixen to wreck up the place but ends up plumb tuckered out on his bed." He took off his cowboy hat and fiddled with the tassel. The corners of his eyes were wet with tears. "I hate it... god, damn it."

"Boone! That's no way for a little boy to talk."

"I don't care! It's the god-honest truth. I can't stand my father when he's a loco-son-of-a-bitch."

"Boone!" Phoebe's voice was firm and threatening. "One more word and I'll have to wash out your mouth with soap. I won't tolerate this sort of sailor-talk in my household." She got up, about to leave the room. "Now, I'm gonna get to the bottom of this."

"No! You can't!" Boone exclaimed, running after her. "He's not the same when he's drunk. Please, Phoebe, I don't want you getting' hurt."

"I'll be fine."

Crash!

"Phoebe!" Boone clung to her leg, hiding his face in her skirt.

Crash!

Slowly, she tiptoed out of the room to find Clayton struggling to climb the stairs. At the moment, it looked like he had given up, splayed across the steps with a half-empty bottle of whiskey in his hand.

Suddenly, that bottle went flying across the room. It crashed against the wall. Pieces of glass flew in every direction.

Phoebe flinched. Boone trembled against her.

"Why'd you have to leave me?" Clayton's words were so muddled that Phoebe could barely understand what he was saying. "I needed you, dammit!" He hung his head in his hand. "Rebecca..."

Boone's mother, Phoebe thought.

"Does he do this often?" She asked in a whisper.

Boone simply clung to the fabric of her skirt, refusing to budge.

"Boone, answer me." She took him by the shoulders and held him at arm's length. "Please, I need to know."

"Only on Saturdays..."

"I see. Go on to your room. Everything's going to be okay, I promise."

"But... I'm scared." His bottom lip quivered as he spoke. "Please..."

"Go to your room." She insisted.

Hesitantly, he did as he was told. Once she heard the soft thud of his door, she took a deep breath, trying to steady her nerves. She could sympathize with the little boy. After all, her father had been a belligerent drunk all her life. She had spent most of her childhood hiding from him underneath her bed.

She wasn't about to let Boone go through the same trauma.

"Clayton." She called out at the top of the stairs. "What in tarnation do you think you're doing? Do you have any idea what time it is?"

Clayton cocked his head to the side, staring into the distance like he wasn't quite sure where her voice was coming front.

"Let's get you into bed, shall we?" With her heart beating fast, she stepped down and hooked her arm underneath his, hoisting him back on his feet. He stumbled forward, nearly losing his balance but she managed to keep him steady.

He blinked, vision blurry as he looked at his new wife. A toothy smile swept across his features. "Why hello there, you're as pretty as a little red heifer."

"That's no way to talk to your wife," Phoebe spoke through gritted teeth. The compliment stung her like a wasps' sting. Did this man only want her for her beauty? After all, drunken words speak sober thoughts.

"You ain't my wife." He spat, jerking away from her. He reeled back, losing his footing.

Crash!

Phoebe's eyes nearly bugged out of her skull.

Her husband was laying, motionless, at the bottom of the stairs.

Chapter 4

When Clayton woke up, the throbbing in his temples felt like someone was taking a sledgehammer to his head – repeatedly.

He groaned, about to get up when someone pressed down on his shoulders. "What in Sam hill...?"

"Quiet," Phoebe said, voice firm. "Stay still." Gently, she poured disinfectant onto a rag and dabbed the cut on his forehead.

"Ouch!" Clayton's eyes shot open with the pain. "What on earth are you doing to me?"

"Quit your bellyaching."

He furrowed his brows in confusion. "Phoebe?"

"Mhm." She pursed her lips together as she prepared the bandages, cutting them into even strips.

"What happened?"

"You drank yourself into a goddamn stupor last night, that's what."

"Where's Boone."

"Playing by the stables. I told him to give us some space. I need to have a word with you."

Clayton once again tried to get up.

This time, Phoebe helped him into a sitting position, placing a couple of pillows behind his back.

"I'm really sorry. Things got a little out of hand at the saloon. Bets were made. A good friend o' mine walked in."

"That's no excuse to scare your child half to death." Phoebe rolled the bandages around his head, making sure they were nice and tight. "Not to mention, you nearly made me a widow."

A dark cloud settled overhead at the mention of the word 'widow.' His eyes become dull and lackluster. "Rebecca."

Phoebe took his hands in hers. "Look, I can't imagine how hard it must be to lose a wife. I understand that you must miss her an awful lot. But, you can't let her death ruin that rest of your life. You remarried to give your son the family he deserves now pull your part and start acting like a responsible father." She reached forward and cupped his cheek in her palm, drawing him closer to her.

Naturally, their faces gravitated together. She looked into her eyes and felt her heart quicken. She hadn't known this man for very long but she knew, without a doubt, that deep down, he was a good man – an honest man.

"Please, you must let go of the past and move on..." She whispered as she leaned in. For the first time, their lips brushed together.

Clayton felt a stirring in his chest that he hadn't felt in a long, long time. Losing himself in the moment, he wrapped his arms around her waist and pulled her into the bed with him. Their kiss intensified as he relaxed into her warmth.

She ran her fingers through his thick hair, cheeks flushed with excitement.

Their lungs started to burn but still, they continued their intimate embrace. Clayton refused to let go of her, addicted to the taste of her sweet, sweet lips. His heart thrummed like a racehorse. Any second and it would explode out of his chest. But he didn't care. At least he would die a happy man.

Phoebe's head became as light as a feather. Her body weightless and free. She felt like she could spring into the air and fly.

Finally, they broke away from the kiss and gazed into each other's eyes. "Thank you." Clayton ran his thumb across her cheek. "I needed someone to knock some sense into me." He planted a kiss on the tip of her nose. "I promise to be the husband you deserve."

Phoebe smiled. "I know you will."

***

The couple walked out to the stables later that afternoon to find Boone tending to the horses.

"He's incredible," Phoebe commented.

"He is." Clayton agreed with a nod.

They watched for a little while longer as Boone carried the horse feed from the barrels over to each individual stall. He'd take his time talking to the horses and running his hand along their muzzle. "Gone grow up to become a cowboy, just like his old grandpap."

"Oh?" Phoebe asked.

Clayton grinned. "Oh, my pap is a local legend, he is. I reckon the whole country knows his name. Levi Swift. Fastest rider this side of the Mississippi. Always rode bareback, too."

"Does Boone know how to ride?" Phoebe tucked in a few loose strands of hair back into her bonnet. She blushed, recalling the time she had just spent with Clayton. It was the first time she had felt like a married woman.

And, oh, it felt glorious.

"Not quite. I've been hesitant about teaching him since he can't see n' all."

"It can't hurt to try." She said as she stepped forward.

Boone stopped what he was doing and looked in her direction. "Phoebe?"

"And your father."

Boone frowned. He kicked his heels into the dirt and clenched his hands into tight fists. He hadn't forgiven his father for the previous night.

Phoebe lowered herself to his level and placed a hand on his shoulder. "Don't worry, I had a word with him. He won't be drinking again, I promise."

His eyebrows lifted. "Really?"

"Mhm."

Suddenly, the little boy flew forward and hugged her tight. "Thank you!"

She ruffled up his hair in an affectionate manner. Phoebe never imagined how rewarding it would be to act as someone's mother.

Already, she felt an extreme tenderness toward the little boy and she knew she'd do whatever it took to make him happy. "Now, what do you say we go on a ride."

"Ride?" Boone repeated. "Where are we going?"

"Nowhere in particular." She looked back at Clayton. "Your father and I believe it's high time for you to learn how to ride a horse on your own."

"What, really?" Boone's jaw hung agape. He couldn't believe it. "But, paw, you always said –"

"Forget what I said. You're a Swift. And Swifts all know how to ride like the back of their hand. You'll be no exception." And with that, he picked up his son and placed him on the back of his most reliable stallion.

Chapter 5

Boone was a fast learner. By nightfall, he had already figured out how to make the horse respond to his every touch and tug.

Tuckered out, the little boy passed out in his bed the second his father tucked him in.

Meanwhile, Phoebe milled about in the kitchen, brewing a fresh pot of tea. As she waited for the kettle to boil, she rummaged through the cabinets and discovered Clayton's stash of liquor bottles. One by one, she poured them out the window.

When Phoebe turned around to grab the last one, Clayton was standing there, holding it in his hands.

She studied his face, waiting for him to decide.

He looked up at her and smiled at her. "I don't need this." And he threw it out the window. "I'm a man of my word, you best believe that." Without another word, he picked up his wife and sat her down on the kitchen table. Gently, he kissed the side of her neck. "You're the answer to my prayers."

Phoebe shook her head. "No. I'm just a girl from Vermont."

"Oh, you're much more than that." He said with a grin.

Phoebe shivered. His intentions were as clear as day, painted into his eyes.

"And now you're mine."

***

The following Saturday.

"Atta boy, Boone. That's what I want to see!" Clayton cheered as his son galloped around the circuit, a bright smile on his face. "That there is a real Swift."

"Ah, there you are." Phoebe walked up to her husband with a pitcher of lemonade and a couple of cups. "I was wondering what trouble you two were getting yourselves into."

"No trouble at all." Clayton kissed his wife and smiled. "He's really getting the knack of it."

Phoebe nodded. She could tell that Boone was a born natural. The way he moved, it was like he was a part of the horse – like they were speaking some secret language that only they could understand.

Clayton wrapped his arm around her waist. "They're having a little jamboree in town. How about we have us some fun tonight?"

"No drinking?"

"Nah, only dancin'. You have my word." He winked. "Tell you what, if you catch me with a drink in my hand, feel free to shoot me."

Phoebe chuckled. "You have better luck with Boone making the shot. I've never held a gun before."

"Never?" Clayton asked, eyes widening with surprise. "Oh, we'll have to change that. It's a wild place out here. Never know what'll happen. Bandits. Red skins. Coyotes. You name it. I want my wife to be able to protect herself if I'm not around."

"Tonight, let's just stick to dancing."

***

And that's exactly what they did. With Boone safe and sound with a relative, the new couple was free to do as they pleased.

The band played a high-beat swing that echoed through the wooden floorboards.

Phoebe kicked off her shoes, hitched her skirt, and let her hair down.

Clayton held her close. Phoebe was one hell of a woman and he wasn't about to let one of these two-bit varmints lay a finger on her. He could tell they were staring at her, too. Their eyes glowed with greed as they licked their chops.

He only held her closer, bodies pressed so close he could feel the beating of her heart.

"Clayton!" She squealed when he bent her backward, forcing her to kick her leg into the air.

He chuckled. "What is it darlin'? Have you never danced the two-step before?" With a charming smile, he guided her through the motions, his movements so fluid it felt like they were gliding across the dancefloor.

Phoebe smiled wider than a wheelbarrow as the world spun round and round. Her heart thumped louder than a drum but she didn't care. This was one of the best nights of her life.

"Hey! Clay! Take a load off and tip a couple back with us." Clayton's drinking mates hollered at him.

He ignored them and continued to dance.

"Oh, come on, Clay. Your ears aren't stuffed with cow cud, are they?" They hackled with laughter, slapping the bar with their hands.

Without a word, Clayton took his wife's hand and walked out with her.

"Are you okay?" Phoebe asked.

"I'm done with that part of my life. I want to become a better man for you – for Boone. I'm not going to let a couple of bottles of whiskey ruin everything. Come on, I want to show you something.'"

"Hmm?"

Before she could get an answer out of him, he hoisted her onto the back of their horse. A second later, he settled in front of her.

She wrapped her arms around him and rested her head on his shoulder.

"Yah!" He yelled, prompting his steed into a gallop.

"Where are we going?"

"You'll see." He answered mysteriously.

After about ten minutes of riding, he slowed into a canter. Up ahead, a large mountain bluff loomed against the skyline. The moon shone brilliantly, painting the landscape in a blanket of silver lighting.

"It's beautiful..." She whispered in awe.

"Not really as beautiful as you and the life we're going to have together."

Epilogue

Two years later.

Phoebe had some exciting news she wanted to share but she couldn't find her family anywhere.

"Mrs. Swift?" Their house maid popped her head out from one of the guest rooms. "The gentleman that's been staying here, he wanted to have a word with you."

"Certainly." Phoebe straightened out her dress before heading down the hall. For the past week, their inn had been home to a group of city-folk. Some sort of college field trip. New Yorkers with nothing better to do, she figured.

Knock. Knock.

She waited by the door as she heard a series of shuffling.

Thud!

"Not there, you idiot! There!" Someone called out.

Phoebe shook her head. These people were such an odd bunch but they paid well and that's what mattered.

Finally, someone answered the door. It was the leader of the group. He pushed his round spectacles up the bridge of his nose as he looked Phoebe over. "Ah, I was just meaning to have a word with you. Please, come in."

Phoebe crossed the threshold and walked into utter disarray. There were pieces of paper scattered all over the floor. Trunks overflowed with clothing. The bed looked like it had gone through a tornado. Despite her best efforts, she couldn't keep the look of disgust from her face.

"My apologies. We'll have this mess straightened out by the time we leave. We're just getting everything prepared for the next leg of our operation."

"Did you find anything worthwhile in Wyoming?" She inquired politely.

"A couple of bones here and there. Nothing I was hoping for." He said with a shake of his head. "But, hopefully, we'll be met with better luck in Arizona. One of my colleagues was just there and he discovered a tremendous find."

Phoebe listened to the college professor, occasionally nodding her head although, in all honesty, she didn't know what paleontologists did or why they were so interested in old bones. Seemed like a waste of time and money.

"Anyway, I just wanted to personally thank you for your generous hospitality. We were here a few years back when it was just your husband and the difference is night and day."

"Thank you, I do my best." Phoebe bowed slightly as she accepted the compliment. It made her feel good that she had bettered her husband's business.

The professor reached into his wallet and pulled out a hefty sum of money. "This is more than I owe but use it toward properly educating that boy of yours. He has potential and a great mind."

Phoebe smiled. "That's very generous of you, sir, but I can't accept this. You'll need it for your trip."

"I insist." He placed the bills in her hand.

Phoebe had no choice but to accept the payment. She nodded her appreciation, pocketed the money, and left the paleontologists to their packing.

Downstairs, she placed the money in a little tin box where they kept their savings. They planned to move into their own home soon so they could have a bit of privacy away from the guests. Already, they were getting close to having enough. Clayton planned to build most of it with his own two hands in order to save them some money. Phoebe was prepared to help in any way necessary even if it meant learning how to hammer in a nail. She wasn't the kind of girl who was afraid to get her hands dirty.

"Betsy, have you seen my husband anywhere?" She asked the cook.

"Hmm, no ma'am. Haven't seen him all morning."

"Strange. Tell the staff I'll be gone for a little while."

"Alright."

Phoebe walked over to the stables. Usually, if she couldn't find her husband inside the inn, he was hiding out with the horses.

Today was no different.

She caught father and son inside a stall helping a mare deliver a couple of fillies. Boone had his features pinched with concentration as he listened to his father's every word and did exactly as he was told.

Soon enough, two healthy horses frolicked around on wobbly legs, tasting the world for the first time.

Clayton straightened his back, wiping the sweat from his brow. "Oh, Feebs, I didn't see you there." He smiled at his wife. "I would kiss you but I'm sort of a mess."

Phoebe's heart started to race. Her mind buzzed as she tried to figure out the best way to tell him the news. Her fingers shook with her nervousness.

What if he wasn't prepared for this next chapter in their lives?

She gulped, feeling like there was a boulder lodged in her throat. Her lips were stuck together like someone had stitched them shut.

"Feebs?"

"I have something I need to tell you..." She said, her voice barely a whisper.

"Mom, is everything okay?" Boone asked, stepping forward. "You sound scared."

"Not scared. Nervous." She admitted.

"You're supposed to leave the nerves to Nelly, here." Clayton chuckled, patting the new mother.

"Well, she's not the only one who's going to be a mother."

It took Clayton a moment to realize what his wife was saying. His eyes widened. "Do you mean...?"

She nodded.

"What?" Boone asked, unable to see the facial expressions of his parents.

Suddenly, Clayton jumped up and let out an overjoyed yelp. He took his wife into his arms and spun her around. "Do you really mean it?"

"Yes!" Phoebe laughed as they fell into a stack of hay.

"What's going on?" Boone demanded, feeling helplessly lost.

The couple stopped. Clayton held Phoebe's hand, squeezing it tightly. "Son, I don't know how to say this..."

"Paw?" Boone blinked, waiting for his father to continue.

Phoebe stepped forward and placed her hand on his shoulder. "What do you think about becoming an older brother?"

"What?"

"We're going to have a baby." Clayton clarified. Instinctually, he placed his hand on Phoebe's stomach. Joy blossomed through his heart making it swell. To have a child with this amazing woman...

Of course, he was nervous. He remembered the terrible experience with Rebecca but, at the same time, he wanted this more than anything.

"I'm going to have a brother?" Boone asked.

Phoebe laughed. "Well, we don't know whether it'll be a boy or a girl, just yet."

"When will you know?"

"When it comes out, I suppose." Clayton chuckled.

Boone smiled from ear to ear. "I'm gonna be the best older brother in Wyoming – no, in the whole wild, wild west – no, in the whole world!" He exclaimed, jumping up and down.

"Yes, you will." Phoebe agreed.

"I'm going to teach it *everything*. Riding. Shooting. Just you wait and see!" Boone paced back and forth listing off all the things he wanted to show his sibling-to-be.

Clayton kissed Phoebe's cheek before nibbling on her earlobe ever so gently. "I love you."

MILEY'S PRAYER

MICHELLE HENRY

Chapter 1

Miley tried to focus on her homework, but she knew that was going to be impossible. Her graduation date from UCLA might be approaching but so was the arrival of her very best friend in the world. When Lauren arrived, she and Miley were going to have an amazing weekend. Miley was in charge of showing her all the touristy sites in LA.

Miley glanced at the clock and calculated the time her friend would need to arrive at her dorm after her flight arrived in LA. She should be coming in less than half an hour. "Come on," Miley said. "Just get here already. It's not like I'm getting any homework done anyway."

When Lauren finally wandered in to the dorm lobby, looking sort of lost, Miley jumped up and embraced her best friend. "Hey!" she said.

Lauren laughed. "Hey to you too! I got pretty lost coming here. As in, I found out I am severely impaired and cannot read road signs at all."

"Hey, you're here. You found the right building. It's perfect. No worries."

Lauren laughed. "Except for the six billion people I cut off trying to get to my exit. Hopefully, I won't see them again during my visit."

Miley waved her hand. "No big deal. Everyone cuts everyone off. They won't remember you as anyone special."

"Oh. . ." Lauren said. "That made me feel a lot better."

"Come on, let's get your stuff up to my dorm room. I finally got permission to have an external guest stay the night here."

"They probably looked up my Facebook profile pic and saw all the danger I could bring," Lauren said, hefting her bag up the stairs.

"Hey, they've put up with me all these years," Miley said. "You can't do anything to scare my RAs that I haven't already tried."

"If that's a challenge, I am more than willing to take you on," Lauren said.

Miley shook her head. "No challenge. No need to prove anything. I just want to catch up on your life."

"There's more to catch up on your life," Lauren said. "You come home to visit every holiday. I've never been to LA to visit."

"Which is super strange considering that your boyfriend is out here more often than not."

Lauren shrugged. "It's not like I can just drop my college classes and fly out to spend all the time in the world with him."

Miley nodded. "I know, but still. Now you get to see his world. But tonight is reserved for me, right?"

"Of course! I haven't made any secretive plans behind your back," Lauren said.

"No, but you just planned to come one of the last weekends before graduation, because you knew you wouldn't have free room and board after that point."

Lauren laughed. "You make it seem so evil. I thought I was being smart."

Miley shook her head. "I have your plans all figured out. Alright. Here we are. This is my dorm room. That's Kaylee's bed over there. We can flip a coin for the hammock and my bed."

"If you don't really want to sleep in the hammock, I would totally take it," Lauren said.

Miley shrugged. "It's yours then. I've slept in it before." Lauren got her things settled in the room, then Miley took her out for hamburgers. The girls enjoyed catching up with each other and making plans for the next day.

"What time do we have to wake up?" Miley asked Lauren.

"If we want to be there at six, we need to wake up at five, at least," Lauren said.

"Is there even one of those in the morning?" Miley asked.

Lauren shook her head and laughed. "Yes. It looks a lot like the five in the evening."

"Except with a lot more pain involved," Miley said. "Fine, I shall be there, only because I've been living in LA this long and never seen a shoot."

"Garret said it's going to go all morning, then they have a break in the afternoon, before they need to be back at night."

"So, are you thinking beach in that time?" Miley asked.

Lauren nodded. "Totally. I didn't bring my bathing suit for nothing."

"Alright," Miley said. "Let's go back to the dorm room. If we're getting up that early, I should try to go to sleep before midnight."

Lauren laughed. "I'm already falling asleep right now, and it's only nine o'clock."

"I'll give you a pass, because you're used to a different time zone," Miley said. "Let me help you to the car, old grandma."

Chapter 2

"What's this movie going to be called?" Miley asked, trying to stay awake as they drove down the highway.

"I can't remember." Lauren pounded her head as she tried to get the name out. "Something with like 'lion' in the name or something. I seriously don't remember. You can ask Garrett."

"And they're going to let two random people on the set?" Miley asked skeptically.

"Garret said we could be there as long as we are quiet. So, I don't see a problem."

"Maybe being quiet for hours on end," Miley laughed. "Come on, I think this is the place you said to park."

They began walking toward the building where the filming would be taking place. Lauren was walking a little faster, and Miley smiled at her anticipation of seeing her boyfriend after so long. They had trouble getting in, but the guy at the door finally let them in. Lauren ran to Garrett.

"Hey, baby!" he said, picking her up and spinning her around. "It's so good to see you."

Lauren kissed him and began talking a mile a minute.

"Hey, wait like an hour, then I'll be off for a little bit while the main actors do a short scene. I promise I'll be all yours."

Lauren laughed and embraced Garrett again. "Okay, I'll just be patient, and wait right here." Garrett acknowledged Miley then turned back to the set.

"Why do they have to be so early?" Miley asked.

"Something about the morning light," Lauren shrugged. "I don't know, but if my director told me to be here, I would be here."

"I think it's cool that they're making a Christian movie," Miley said. "It'll be good to have a movie with romance that doesn't mean the characters have to end up in bed."

Miley's voice trailed off as she saw a man who was speaking to the director. He had short blonde hair, and his face was smoothed and tanned. He was dressed up nicely in black pants and a collared shirt, and Miley couldn't take her eyes away. She wanted to ask Lauren about him; maybe she knew something. But Miley was too entranced watching him pointing to different areas on the script and asking questions. Finally, he turned away and jogged over to Garrett. As the guys began talking, Miley finally made herself look away.

"That guy," she said, indicating the blonde, "is very attractive. You happen to know who he is?"

Lauren shook her head. "Sorry. I'm not on scanning for potential boyfriend duty."

Miley made a face at her friend. "I was just curious," she said, turning away and discreetly following him with her eyes. She was determined to talk with him and see if he was as charming as he was attractive.

After an hour of watching the shots, just as Garrett had promised, he was free for a half hour. He came over, and he and Lauren were talking so quickly that Miley would not have been able to insert herself if she had tried. Besides, she reasoned with herself, it wasn't fair to ask for Garrett's attention for even a moment when he and Lauren had been apart for so long.

Finally, the whole cast got a ten-minute break. Miley saw the blonde standing at a table filled with snacks. She moseyed over and pretending to be busy picking through the options to fill her plate.

"Are you a film student?" the blonde asked her right when their paths were about to cross.

"Me, ah, no, I'm a student, but not of film." Miley cringed at her awkward words. "I'm studying to be a vet."

Miley finally made eye contact, and the blonde was nodding. "An animal lover, then?"

"Yes, that's it."

"So did you just wander into this shooting by mistake?" he asked. "or do you know someone here?"

"My best friend is dating Garrett. I'm sure you know him, he's. . ."

"Yes, old Garrett. Everybody knows him," the blonde said with a smile. "He is the clown of the set."

Miley smiled and nodded. That sounded just like Garrett. "Anyway, I'm just hanging out with my best friend, watching you guys. I'm learning a lot about how movies are made."

"I'm Cameron, by the way," the blonde said, extending his hand.

Miley took it. "Miley," she nodded with a smile. "Nice to meet you."

"And you as well. Are you planning on hanging out all day?"

"Pretty much," Miley said. "But Garrett said we have the afternoon off, so I'm sure I'll be showing Lauren the sights then."

Cameron nodded. "Sounds like fun. Talk to you later. I'd better get back on set."

As Cameron walked away, Miley did not feel any less impressed with him. He was attractive and worth talking to. And judging by the set, he was probably a Christian too. Miley wondered what kind of maneuvering she would have to do to get Garrett to invite Cameron along for their afternoon out.

Turns out, she had someone fighting for her. When she reached Lauren again, Lauren was smiling at her. "Who was that guy?" she asked.

Miley rolled her eyes and faked annoyance, but really she wanted to recount every detail of their encounter. "His name is Cameron. He basically wanted to know if I was lost and what I was doing here."

Lauren laughed. "Well, you can either kill me or thank me. But I saw you guys talking, and I told Garrett he should invite him to come to the beach with us this afternoon."

"You didn't?!" Miley exclaimed before clapping her hands over her mouth. The set director didn't exactly appreciate loud background noises.

Lauren nodded. "I did. I thought you might feel like a third wheel. I mean, of course I would never do anything to exclude you, but I haven't seen Garrett since Christmas, and I've seen you at least twice since then, so you know. . ."

Miley nodded. "I get it. And, thanks. That just made my job a whole lot easier."

"What? Were you going to invite him yourself?" Lauren asked.

Miley nodded, keeping her laughter quiet. "So, thanks. I can't wait for this afternoon."

Chapter 3

The crew all had lunch on set, and Lauren sat with Garrett. The two spent the time trying to catch up on every little detail. Cameron was across the room, hanging out with a couple of guys. He never even came over to say hi to them.

Finally, as lunch was ending, Cameron came over. "I'm going back to my apartment to pick up my bathing suit. Where should I meet you guys?"

Garrett and Cameron came up with a meeting place, and they started moseying their way there, since they already had their bathing suits.

"This whole filming life is so messed up," Miley commented. "You start at six in the morning, then you have a long afternoon break. Why not just start later?"

"It has to do with the lighting," Garrett explained. "Sometimes, it has to do with when we can rent the set." He shrugged. "It can be frustrating, but I have to keep the bigger picture in mind."

Lauren took Garrett's hand, and as they strolled along, Miley agreed. She was glad her friend had invited Cameron. Because if she hadn't, Miley might never have gotten up the nerve to do it herself. After they had walked along the street and Lauren had exclaimed at every aspect of it, they finally came to the little corner store where they would be meeting Cameron.

"How well do you know Cameron?" Miley started asking, fishing for information.

Garrett smiled and pulled Miley into a hug. "If you are trying to be all sly and get info about my friend, then I'm afraid I've figured you out. Just hang out with him and make your own judgment."

"Thanks for all the help," Miley said, removing Garrett's arm from around her shoulders. Just then, Miley saw Cameron striding toward them; he was wearing brightly colored swim shorts and a tank top that left his arm muscles available for viewing.

"You guys ready?" he asked. Miley and Garrett took the lead, hand in hand. Cameron and Miley were left to follow behind.

"What do you normally do on your breaks?" Miley asked Cameron.

He shrugged. "Depends. Since I started working on the set, I seem to have had a lot more of my family and friends interested in visiting me."

Miley laughed. "How long have you been doing movies?"

"Oh, this is my first one," Cameron said. "I mean, I've played minor, extra-type roles in other movies. But, this is the first movie where I am really getting a taste of the acting life."

"What does it taste like?" Miley teased.

"Like early morning hours and lots of memorization."

"Did you want to go into acting?" Miley asked, genuinely curious.

Cameron shrugged. "I don't know. I came here to study, but honestly, I never really thought I would land a role. I think having this role in a Christian movie is even better for my real debut. So, enough about me, what are you doing in LA?"

"I go to UCLA," Miley answered. "My friend Lauren is visiting, so we're doing everything we can to keep us away from studying this weekend."

Cameron smiled, and Miley noticed a dimple in his right cheek. "So going to the beach with two handsome actors is your idea of study distraction?"

Miley laughed. "Wouldn't you agree? Besides, I always pour so much into my studies that I never really take the time to go down to the beach and enjoy myself. It sometimes seems like just a waste of time and a distraction."

"Sometimes, study breaks are just what you need to charge you up for more," Cameron said. Miley shrugged, distracted as the beach came into view.

"Whoa!" Lauren exclaimed. "Look at those waves! I haven't been to the beach since I was a little girl."

"Go get it, woman!" Miley called, her voice chasing after Lauren as she pulled Garrett along. Miley laughed. "Lauren is so free-spirited."

"Now I know why you two are best friends," Cameron said.

"What? I'm not free-spirited," Miley protested. "I'm more like, I have to focus and achieve my goals."

Cameron shrugged. "I see you as free-spirited, and I am entitled to my opinion."

"Come on," Miley said. "That water looks nice and cool." She kicked off her sandals and hopped back and forth on the hot sand as she removed her cover-up. Then, she and Cameron raced down to the water to join their friends.

"Oooh!" Miley squealed as the water splashed up in her face. "This water is really cold."

"Wave!" Garrett called. All four dove under.

When they came up, Miley brushed her hair out of her face. "I need to come to the beach more often," she said to no one in particular.

"I'm pretty sure commandment number eleven in Exodus chapter twenty says 'Do not forgo beach visits when you live within walking distance.'"

Miley laughed. "If you can show me proof of that, I'll make sure I don't disobey anymore."

Cameron shrugged. "Sorry, I didn't bring my Bible into the ocean with me today."

Miley dove under another wave. "Are you a good swimmer?" she asked when she popped back up.

Cameron nodded. "I have been compared to a fish occasionally. But that may have just been referring to how I smell."

Miley began laughing so hard that a wave came out of nowhere and filled her mouth with salt water. She began coughing up the water, and Cameron helped by pounding on her back.

"Gee, joking in the ocean should be a criminal offense," Miley said. "You could have literally committed murder."

Cameron laughed. "Now, you're guilty too," he said. Miley couldn't help but smile whenever Cameron did. He was so handsome and kind and funny that Miley wanted to spend the rest of the day with him. She started imagining what life would be like with Cameron.

"Wave!" Cameron said, calling Miley back to the present. She jumped the wave, letting it carry her backwards a few feet. By this point, Garrett and Lauren had drifted a short way away. For all practical purposes, Miley and Cameron were alone.

"Are you going to act forever?" Miley asked.

Cameron shrugged. "I don't know. If this movie does well, it might give me a stepladder into doing other movies. I don't think I could get a lead in a secular movie, though. There are too many others fighting for those spots. I don't mind. I'll take smaller roles for now. But yeah, I hope I can keep doing this forever."

"So you like living in LA?" Miley asked.

"Yes, that's why I live here. Do you not like it?"

"I come from a smaller town, so the traffic amazes me pretty much every day."

Cameron laughed. "That's okay. I've been living here since I was fifteen, and it still amazes me."

Miley smiled, admiring his dimple. The water lifted her up and carried her very close to him. "Sorry," she said. "The water has a mind of its own." She took a few steps back so that she was facing the ocean again and giving Cameron his own space.

They continued talking, and Cameron checked his watch. "I should probably go soon. I wouldn't want to be late even though this has been really fun."

Miley nodded. "Of course."

"Do you know where Garrett is? I'm sure he's lost track of time."

"I think he and Lauren are laying out on the beach."

"Alright, are you coming out with me?" Cameron asked. He glanced back at the heavy waves building behind them.

"Yeah, I might as well," Miley said. "I'm hungry, and I'm sure Lauren is too."

Miley followed Cameron out of the water, and the wind immediately whipped at her body. She wrapped her towel around her and waited as the others gathered up their things.

"Are you guys going straight from here to the set?" Lauren asked.

"I brought clothes to change, and they have showers," Garrett said. "Go get something to eat, and meet us there when you can."

Lauren nodded and took a few steps away with Garrett to say goodbye to him. Miley turned to Cameron with a smile, intending to make a joke about her friend. Instead, she was met with a surprise. Cameron placed his arm around her waist, pulled her closer, and slowly leaned his head down to her. He kissed her gently. The kiss lasted only a few moments, but it was so soft. Miley opened her eyes and bit her lip, trying to hide the smile that wanted to take over her face.

"I hope to see you later," Cameron said.

Miley nodded. "I'll be on set tonight."

"Goodbye," Cameron gave Miley one more kiss on the cheek. Cameron started walking in the direction of the set. Garrett caught up to him a few minutes later. Miley turned to Lauren with the biggest smile on her face.

"What? What happened?" Lauren asked.

Chapter 4

The two friends ordered some food before they headed back to the set. Neither one of them wanted to miss a moment of fun. "I can't believe he kissed you," Lauren said as they sat over their dinner.

Miley couldn't stop smiling. "I know! I mean, I was feeling the attraction. How could I not? Besides his good looks, he's really funny. I was laughing probably 80% of the time we were together. Then when he kissed me, I was like, this is it! He is a great man, and he likes me."

Lauren smiled. "I'm so happy for you guys. But if you decide to live out here, then I still expect yearly visits."

"Don't get the cart before the horse," Miley said. "I just met him today. I know how I feel, and I'm pretty sure I know how he feels, but. . ."

"Don't let any 'buts' creep in," Lauren advised. "Believe in the magic of it, and it won't go away. Come on, let's go over to the set."

Miley brought an extra croissant with her, just in case she got hungry later. The kind of snacks they offered for the actors were a bit too healthy for her. Sometimes, a girl just wanted some grain and chocolate.

They settled into some comfy chairs and watched the actors out of the corner of their eyes. "I don't know how they do it," Lauren said. "I'm tired after all afternoon in the ocean. I feel like I could just fall asleep any second. Yet, there they are acting as though nothing happened."

"I know," Miley agreed. "I'm pretty tired too, but I guess they have to do what they have to do. If I had to study tonight, I would be doing it whether or not I wanted to."

"Good point," Lauren said. "Look, I'm just going to lay on the floor here and doze a little. Wake me up if anything interesting happens. I just want to talk to Garrett one more time, then maybe we can head back to your room."

"Alright, sweet dreams," Miley said, as Lauren snagged a blanket from somewhere and curled up on the floor. Miley shook her head. Her friend was so comfortable with herself. Only she could fall asleep while watching actors film for a movie. Miley was too interested in watching Cameron act out his part. He was playing the part of a husband. His wife had been unfaithful, and Cameron was trying to work through the problem. The scenes weren't filmed in order, and that kept Miley a bit confused throughout the whole production.

Suddenly, Miley froze. There was Cameron putting his arm around his "wife's" waist just as he had done to Miley not two hours earlier. He was leaning down! Miley's stomach clenched as Cameron kissed the woman just as he had kissed Miley earlier that day. Miley couldn't watch him, but she couldn't look away either. He slowly kissed her. Miley rubbed her lips together. No! How could he do that?! Clearly, kissing didn't mean anything to him.

Miley felt close to crying. The director gave directions, and the couple froze in place, lips connected while the camera moved around them. Finally, they were released from each other. Miley quickly found something interesting to study on the floor. No way was she going to let Cameron see how much it had affected her.

When she looked up again, they were beginning the same scene once more. Miley stood up and walked out. She couldn't sit there and watch as Cameron kissed that woman again and again. Why had she thought that she would mean something to him after only a day?

Miley waited outside, calming herself and praying for patience. What should she do? She needed to convince Lauren that they should go back to her dorm room right then. At least Miley wouldn't be forced to witness such humiliation over and over again.

Miley entered the set again and gently shook Lauren who was peacefully sleeping on the floor. "I'm really tired too," Miley whispered. "Let's just go back to my dorm room, while I'm still capable of driving."

Lauren stretched and looked around. "I really want to talk to Garrett first. You can just leave me here. He'll take me to your dorm."

"I don't think that's a good idea," Miley said. "You can wave to him. He'll understand. I know you guys have early plans for tomorrow too."

Lauren nodded slowly. "Yes, I guess. Okay, just give me a couple minutes to wake up."

Miley waited impatiently as her friend stood, stretched, and gathered her things. Lauren took long enough that the crew was given a five-minute break. She ran up to Garrett, kissed him and said goodnight before following Miley out the door. The two girls could barely stay awake for the short drive back to Miley's dorm.

"I can't believe it's already Saturday night," Lauren moped. "This weekend has passed too quickly."

"There's still tomorrow," Miley reminded her friend.

Chapter 5

When Miley woke up Sunday morning, she had had an excellent dream. She wanted to just close her eyes and fall into that dream again. "Miley!" Lauren said. "It's already seven o'clock."

"You say that like it's a bad thing," Miley said. "I'm tired. We had a big day yesterday. Let me sleep."

"I don't want to leave you here by yourself," Lauren said.

"They're not filming today," Miley said.

"Yes, I know, but Garrett was going to take me to his church. I thought you would want to go along."

Miley stretched and answered in the affirmative even though she really wanted to sleep another two hours. "Just get some cereal from my stash and milk from the fridge," Miley directed, slowly beginning her day.

Once she was showered, dressed, and ready, Lauren was practically ready to drag her out the door. "Gee, woman, you are in a hurry," Miley said as she settled into the driver's seat. "What time is the service?"

"Nine."

"We could have picked a later service," Miley said, tuning the radio to a station that was actually playing music.

"Well, we wanted plenty of time for lunch and walk along the Hollywood Walk of Fame before I need to take my flight back."

"I forget how soon that is," Miley said, trying to snap out of her sleepiness. "This weekend has passed too quickly."

"I know. I wish I could have more time, but I have a test on Monday. I need to actually study for it on my flight back."

Miley laughed at her friend. "Good luck with that. I have a feeling that you will be sleeping. Sweet dreams, Lauren."

Lauren laughed. "A girl can aspire to do well, even if that's not what actually happens. Weekends should have a day after Sunday and before Monday so that you can recover from the craziness of a weekend."

"Maybe once you graduate from grad school, you can invent a day like that," Miley suggested.

They parked in front of the church and walked toward the front. Suddenly, Miley stopped. "What is Cameron doing here?"

"Don't look so upset," Lauren replied. "I did it as a favor for you. I figured you would enjoy hanging out with him again. Besides, Garrett says he goes to church here. Garrett only had to invite him to the lunch part."

Miley closed her eyes and took a deep breath. She was not going to argue with her friend right here where the guys could see. Neither would she ruin the last part of their weekend. She would just let this slide and explain everything to Lauren later.

"Come on!" Lauren said, hurrying forward to embrace Garrett. They looked so happy together, that Miley couldn't help feeling a little jealous. How had Lauren found a guy like Garrett who loved her so much? Miley felt like Cameron had been cheating the night before. In a regular relationship, that would never be tolerated, why should she ever put up with anything of the kind in her life?

"Good morning," Cameron said.

Miley gave him a friendly enough nod before focusing on Lauren and where they were going to sit. Miley maneuvered the sitting situation so that she was sitting beside Lauren. Cameron was on the other side of Garrett. Miley was chatting with Garrett and Lauren. Suddenly, Lauren turned toward Miley and made an awkward situation even more awkward.

"We didn't mean to separate you," she said. "Sometimes, I just don't pay attention. Go ahead, you can slide past me so you can sit beside Cameron."

Miley had tried to give her friend the "terminate this" look, but her friend didn't seem to notice anything. Miley obligingly went to her reserved space beside Cameron, but she refused to talk to him. What would she say anyway? *Stop doing your job. It offends me?* She didn't have any claim on Cameron. She'd met him only the day before. That didn't make her situation any easier.

The service started, which left no opportunity for talking. That didn't mean that Lauren and Garrett didn't completely ignore that a few times, but Miley took scrupulous notes, making sure she underlined, circled, and noted everything necessary.

When the service was over, she felt Cameron's hand on her arm. She tried to compose her features, but she was sure there was still a trace of contempt in them. "Yes?" she asked.

"Are you okay?" Cameron asked. "You seem totally different than you were yesterday."

Miley pasted a smile on her face. "I'm completely fine. I'm just tired. You know, this weekend has been a tad bit busier than the majority of my weekends are."

"Ah, yeah, I get that. I'm sure you have studies to attend to today anyway."

"Ready, guys?" Garrett asked as they emerged from the church and entered the parking lot. "I'm am starving."

"It's 10:30," Miley replied with a genuine smile. "You must be perpetually hungry."

"Let's say my breakfast was not of royal standards. Where do we want to eat?"

The group began talking about where they wanted to eat, but Miley didn't really join in. If she could have found a graceful way to abandon her best friend in her last few hours of exploring LA, she would have done so. It's not like Lauren would have even noticed. She was so caught up with Garrett that Miley hadn't talked to her much at all whenever Garrett was in the picture. And Lauren had made sure Garrett was in the picture as much as possible.

Chapter 6

"Hey, Miley, are you okay?" Lauren asked discreetly, looping her hand through her best friend's arm.

"I know you were trying to think of me and be kind inviting Cameron. But maybe I'm not interested in him."

"Hold on, girl!" Lauren said, turning to face her friend completely. "Just yesterday you were thanking me profusely for doing the same thing I did today. Now you're like how could you do such a thing? What happened, Miley?"

Miley shrugged. "It was fine. Thanks, honestly. But I just didn't. . .want to waste my whole weekend with some guy when I could be spending it with you."

"Aw," said Lauren. "It's okay. Honestly, I've enjoyed these double dates, if we can call them that. Let's go enjoy our last few hours and eat something delicious."

Miley smiled and headed toward her car. Cameron was put in her car so that Lauren could ride with Garrett. Miley opened the windows and let the wind stream through the car so that talking wouldn't be so easy. When they pulled up in front of the restaurant they had finally picked, Miley rolled up the windows and slowly brushed out her hair.

"Something is definitely wrong," Cameron said. He reached over and took the keys out of their position in the ignition. "And I refuse to give you your keys until you tell me."

"So you are taking to the path of theft?"

Cameron shrugged. "If that's what it takes. I'm just not understanding. Everything seemed fine. We shared a great day yesterday." Cameron smiled slowly. "We even shared a great kiss. I don't get why you're so angry. Or is it not with me but with something else?"

Miley shrugged and looked out the window at the restaurant. Lauren and Garrett were just getting out. "We should probably go inside. They'll be waiting for us," she said, pointing at the restaurant.

Cameron shrugged. "I think this is more important right now. I just want to know if I did something wrong. If I did, maybe I can fix it."

Miley shook her head. "Honestly, I really don't want to talk about it. Let's just get through today, then Lauren will go back to Colorado, and I won't need to see either you or Garrett for a very long time."

"You don't want to see me again?" Cameron asked. He didn't ask it in one of those 'Please feel sorry for me and do what I want' kind of ways but more along the lines of simply being confused.

Lauren waved to them from the curb. Miley waved back and held up one finger to indicate that she would be coming in just a minute. "I think it's better if we don't see each other again." Miley held her hand out for her key, cracking her door open at the same time.

"I don't agree," Cameron said. "The day we had yesterday was amazing. I don't just go around kissing women for no reason. I meant that kiss, and I wanted to kiss you because I thought we were building something."

Miley shook her head, bitterness rising. "It's funny you should say that. Because I think you do go around kissing random women. Not an hour after you kissed me on the beach, I go back to the set and see you kissing another woman. Do you think that was fun to watch? Do you think that was something I enjoyed? Sure you don't go around kissing women. . ."

"That's not fair!" Cameron protested. "That's my job. That kiss didn't mean anything."

"Oh, but what about the fifty kisses after that?"

Cameron shook his head. "I said they don't mean anything, and it's true. It's part of my job, but that's the only kissing scene in the whole movie."

"Maybe this movie," Miley replied bitterly. "What about the next movie? Maybe they'll have you in bed with a woman. After all, it doesn't mean anything."

Cameron shook his head. "I wouldn't agree to doing something like that. Honestly, Miley, I'm completely serious when I say it doesn't mean anything."

"Well, it does to me," Miley said. "To me, every kiss means something. You can't just go around kissing anyone you want to kiss. It might hurt the next girl who's interested in you."

Miley opened her door, got out, and closed the door behind her. It didn't matter that he had the key. He would give it to her eventually. Miley didn't feel ready to enter the restaurant either, though. So she just walked around to the back and found a bench to sit on. She wasn't going to allow herself to cry. She wouldn't.

About fifteen minutes later, Miley saw a pair of shoes standing in front of her. She knew they were Cameron's. "May I sit?" he asked. Miley slowly assented.

He didn't say anything. He just put his arm around her shoulders and pulled her closer to him. "I'm sorry, Miley," he said after a few minutes. That was when the tears filled her eyes. She had no right to be putting demands on him. She had just met him. Yes, she was attracted to him. Yes, she wasn't sure she could change that. But, that didn't mean she had the right to make him change his whole life.

"I'm sorry too," Miley said. "It's not like you're just going out kissing random women. It is part of your job."

"It's hard to get," Cameron said, his other hand on her knee. "I know. But really, it doesn't mean anything to me. It's not like when I kissed you yesterday. That kiss made me want more."

Miley looked up at Cameron. "Really?"

"Didn't you feel the same?" he asked.

"Yes," Miley answered. "I really like you."

"Can I kiss you again?"

Miley nodded, turning her lips up toward his. When she had finished kissing him, the smile on Miley's face was all too genuine. "Let's go inside and enjoy Lauren's last few hours," he said.

THE LOST COWBOY

TESS DRISKEL

Chapter One

When Jenny had told people back home that she was moving to Texas for a teaching job, they'd all thought she was crazy. Most of her friends who were finishing college were settling down near home, in the same little towns that they'd all grown up in. Everyone wanted to know why she thought she had to go halfway across the country for a teaching job. Rosewood Elementary, right up the street from her parents, was hiring since Mrs. McKay was retiring, and they'd love to have Jenny.

As if.

It wasn't that Jenny hated the place, that was the thing. There was so much beauty to a northeast winter, and she still appreciated how everyone knew everyone back home. At any of the local shops if they asked her how she was, they generally cared what her answer was. And since there's only been 51 people in her high school graduating class, they'd all known one another well, and they'd all gone off to college together (at least, the 49% of them who went to college).

But she had wanted something more. She wanted to settle down with a guy who she hadn't known since they were scraping their knees playing ball hockey in the street. All the guys in Apex seemed to still think of her as the flat-chested teen with the bad haircut that she'd been in her high school yearbook. She wanted someone who saw who she was now. She wanted to start a family someday, and she wanted her kids to have the best education and other opportunities possible—and she knew that Apex could never offer them the best.

Yet, in her two months in Texas, she'd begun to agree that she must have been crazy in coming there.

The thing was, she hadn't expected it would be this *difficult* to try and find her place somewhere else in her own country. Sure, she knew there were people teaching abroad in China or Japan or other places in the world—she was sure positions like that came with their share of difficulties. But Texas was...Texas. There were grocery stores and her colleagues spoke English and she didn't need to worry about the banks switching off her debit card and...

She slumped behind her desk, fighting back foolish tears at the end of another long work day.

It seemed that every day ended like this lately. It wasn't her first teaching job—she'd done a couple practicums during college—but she couldn't seem to connect with these kids here in Texas...and she certainly couldn't seem to get them to respect her!

In this class, sixth-graders, there was one ringleader, and she knew if she could just get him to behave, the rest of them would follow. But instead, every single day, she saw her lessons totally derailed. He either told jokes or faked snoring or... Well, he seemed to have no end of ways to drive her up the wall. And the rest of the kids just mimicked him. And if she scolded him, half the time he'd mimic her. And then the rest of the kids would follow.

It wasn't as though she could send the entire sixth-grade class to the principal's office. But the rest of the sixth-grade teachers didn't seem to be having any similar problems; instead, they all claimed their kids were darlings: their final year of good behavior before they became the dreaded seventh- and eighth-graders.

There was a knock at the door, and Jenny hastily wiped the tears from her eyes before standing up. "Hi," she said to the (admittedly handsome) man who walked into the room. "Can I help you?"

The brunette man smiled crookedly at her and held out a hand. "You must be Ms. Pritchard—Jenny, is it?" the man drawled, taking her hand in a firm grip. "Now, I know parent-teacher conferences aren't for a few more weeks, but I couldn't help but stop by." He grimaced a little. "I'm Victor Leonards; Mikey Leonards is my son."

Jenny bit her lower lip, dropping her eyes to the floor. Mikey was the trouble-maker in her class. All she could assume was that her student had complained about his latest punishment—that day, she hadn't allowed him to go out to recess with the rest of the class—and that Victor was here to chew her out over it. She couldn't even deal with the students; entitled parents were something else...

"Aww, hey," Victor said, taking a step forward and tapping her chin to get her to look up. He was still smiling gently at her. "I know, I know, Mikey's a bit of a nightmare, isn't he?" He shook his head. "I'd love to make excuses and beg you to forgive him—he's just feeling a bit neglected because we moved right at the start of the school year and he's feeling like everyone else is friends and he's on the outside. But that wouldn't be fair to you, either. I know you're trying your best with him, and from some of the boastful stories he's told his Aunt Cecile, I assume you're having a pretty rough time with him. So I really just wanted to apologize."

Jenny frowned at him, waiting for there to be some sort of catch. "You came all this way to apologize?" she asked suspiciously.

Victor chuckled. "Sure did, Ms. Pritchard." He shrugged broadly. "I can't say things have been easy for me either since Mikey's mother passed. He's a very...strong-willed child." He grinned at her and stage-whispered, "That means, he's a *brat*."

Jenny cracked a smile, though she knew that as a teacher, she shouldn't be agreeing with him—she should come up with some sort of clever, politically-correct thing to say in response, instead. But she couldn't help nodding along with him. She matched Victor's shrug with her own, feigning nonchalance. "We'll get there, though," she said, promising herself as much as she was promising him. "There's still a lot of time left in the school year."

"If there's anything I can do to help..." Victor said, trailing off.

Jenny's eyes lit up with a dangerous glint. "Well, as a matter of fact..."

Victor groaned, covering up a teasing grin, and put his hands over his face. "Oh Lord, what have I got myself into?"

"I need another chaperone for next week's trip to the science museum," Jenny said. "I was going to take this to the PTA and see if there was anything they could do, but if you're volunteering..." It would be perfect if he agreed to go along, she figured: Mikey wouldn't dare act out with his father present, and that meant it would be smooth sailing all day. As it was, she was pretty concerned about how the trip would go.

Victor snorted. "Free work, eh? What day is it again—Wednesday?"

"Thursday, actually. Gives the kids time to go on the trip and then a day to discuss on Friday before they go off home for the weekend."

Victor grimaced. "I'd need to try and shift some things in my schedule," he said, shaking his head. "I run a ranch a little ways outside of town, and our shipments of hay and everything else usually come in on Thursday. And we're short-staffed at the moment, so I really need to be there to supervise their delivery..."

Jenny felt her face fall, but she tried to keep her fake smile in place. "Well, sure, Mr. Leonards," she said sweetly. "I understand. Like I said, I'll just ask the PTA if there's anything they can do. It's no problem."

"Hey, Ms.—*Jenny*. Jenny, it's not that I don't want to help," Victor said earnestly, reaching out and placing a hand on her arm. "I mean, when I say we're short-staffed—at the moment, it's just Mikey and me there at the ranch, plus we get some help from the girls who stable their horses there. But times have been hard lately and we aren't stabling many horses, so that means we can't afford to have extra help come in. If the trip weren't on a Thursday, you could count on me, 100%."

"It's fine, I understand," Jenny said wearily. "It's just been so tough around here, getting used to living her and the school and everything else..." She shook her head. "But that's not something you need to hear. Listen, if anything else comes up, I'll let you know. Otherwise, I appreciate the apology"–whatever it was worth–"and I hope you have a great evening."

"How about this?" Victor asked, giving her a good once-over. "Why don't Mikey and I have you over for supper? Cecile has made a good slow-cook pork this afternoon, so there will be more than enough to go around. And maybe if you and Mikey meet outside the classroom, he'll respect you a bit more than as just his stuffy teacher—no offense."

Jenny frowned, thinking it over. She wondered if there was any sort of rule against going over for dinner at one of her students' houses...? But it wasn't like she was going on a date with Victor or anything like that. It couldn't hurt, could it? Finally, she smiled hesitantly. "That would be nice," she said. She cleared her throat. "Actually, I'd really appreciate that—I have to do my grocery shopping, but I'm hoping I can push it off until the weekend!"

Victor chuckled and offered her his arm. "Well in that case, let's get you out of here so you can relax a little."

Chapter Two

Jenny hadn't really expected dinner with Victor and Mikey to solve any of her troubles with Mikey at school—but she hadn't really expected it to make things worse either. Yet, when faced with the facts at the end of the following week...

She crumpled up the mean notes she'd found on the floor at the end of the day—notes that clearly had been left there for her to find. They had been passed back and forth between two of the students, and they talked about how horrible her classes were, how all their other teachers were more interesting, how ugly she was...

She recognized the handwriting. The student saying the meanest things was Mikey. The person mostly agreeing with him—although occasionally interjecting something as well—was Brian.

"Uh oh, that's a long face for a Friday afternoon," Victor said from the doorway. "What's my trouble-maker son been up to today?"

Jenny sighed but pasted on a fake smile. "Nothing—he's been just lovely, don't worry. I'm just tired. End of the week, you know."

"Why don't I believe you?" Victor asked, pushing off the doorframe with one shoulder and striding into the room. He took the crumpled sheet of paper from her hands, straightening it out and reading it over. He scowled and then shook his head. "I'm going to have to have a strong word with the boy," he said. "This is absolutely unacceptable."

Jenny reached for the piece of paper. "It's fine, Victor," she said. "It doesn't matter." If he had a talking-to with the boy, things would probably only get worse.

Victor refused to give the piece of paper back, though. "Oh no," he said. "This isn't fine. Trust me, I'll get this sorted out." He grimaced. "I'm sorry you have to keep dealing with this. He's starting to get pretty belligerent around the house, too, if that's any consolation."

"Was there something I could help you with?" Jenny asked, folding her arms across her chest. She just wanted to go home and sleep straight through the weekend. Not that she really had time for that—she had a dozen papers to read, plus lesson-planning for next week, plus... She shook her head.

"I know you're new to town," Victor said, "so I wondered if anyone had told you about tonight's harvest festival."

Jenny frowned and shrugged. "I mean, a couple people mentioned it. To be honest, I'm not really in a festival kind of mood."

"Oh, just humor us," Victor said, grinning at her. "If you miss this, you're going to be the only person in the whole town who stays home tonight. Well, except for Mrs. Landers. But she can't get around very well these days."

Jenny rolled her eyes. "Victor, seriously–"

"Oh no," he said, holding up both his hands to stall her protests. "Now, I'm not taking 'no' for an answer. You're coming with me to the harvest festival."

"What even *is* the harvest festival?" Jenny asked wearily. "Like, bobbing for apples and hay mazes and stuff? No scary costumes, right?"

"Oh it's very traditional," Victor said, his eyes sparkling. "There's plenty of food—it's a pot luck, but I've made enough to be from both of us, so don't you worry about that. And there's square-dancing and a bonfire–"

"Square-dancing?" Jenny asked, unable to stop herself. "Is that still a thing? What year do we live in?"

Victor chuckled, a gleam in his eyes. "Is that a challenge—do I need to teach you to have fun?"

Jenny shook her head. "Really, I should get off home. I've got papers to grade, and–"

"Not taking 'no' for an answer," Victor repeated. "If you don't finish the papers, everyone will understand. Just trust me."

Jenny sighed. "I'm not going to be able to get you to leave without me, am I?" she asked.

"Nope!" Victor said cheerfully. "Come on, doll. You'll enjoy it—I promise."

Jenny slowly gathered up everything that she would need to take home for the weekend. "I at least need to swing by my house," she said. "I'm not dressed for a festival."

Victor eyed her jeans and black teeshirt, looking miffed. "You look fine to me. This isn't a formal affair."

"Right," Jenny said patiently. "But it was a lot warmer this morning. I haven't even got a jacket with me. And I don't fancy standing next to the bonfire for the entire night."

"Ah." Victor shrugged off his worn green-and-black flannel and held it out to the teacher. "Here, you can borrow this. I've got a jacket in my truck."

Jenny paused for a moment and then pulled on the flannel, reveling in the warmth left from his body heat. She blushed. "But isn't that..." She shook her head, looking around them. "Victor, I teach your son," she reminded him. "The last thing I need is the whole town thinking..."

"Thinking what?" Victor challenged. "Thinking that I'm a nice guy who lent my flannel to an underdressed school-teacher? Oh woe is me, my secret's out—the town knows I'm nice!"

Jenny sighed. "You really don't think there's anything wrong with this?"

"With what, darling?" Victor asked, ushering her towards the door. "You're new in town, right? Just think of me as the town's ambassador. The mayor was busy."

Jenny snorted. "Fine, fine."

At the festival, they caught up with Mikey and his aunt. Mikey scowled up at her and then turned to his dad. "What is *she* doing here?" he asked snottily.

Victor gave him a stern look. "Jenny—that's Ms. Pritchard to you—is new to town, so I took it upon myself to show her the magic of our harvest festival," he said. "And I'd appreciate your remembering your manners, mister."

Mikey rolled his eyes. "First I have to deal with her all day at school, now I have to deal with her outside of school too? And why is she wearing your flannel? She looks like an elephant."

Jenny tugged self-consciously at the sleeves of the flannel. "Look, maybe I should–"

"Oh no," Victor said, reaching out to catch her arm. "Now you listen up, Mikey—I've had just about enough of your attitude. If you're going to continue to be a brat, I have no problem sending you off home, do you hear me?"

Mikey frowned and kicked at a couple rocks on the ground, but he didn't say anything else.

"Now!" Victor said, clapping his hands together. "Let's go get some grub!"

Chapter Three

Jenny had perhaps had one too many mugs of Alice's hot apple cider, she thought, as Victor wheeled her expertly around the dance floor. Dancing had never really been her strong suit, but Victor somehow kept them both from toppling, and he managed to effortlessly spin her and pull her back into his arms. He was an incredible lead.

He smelled good too. Jenny buried her face against his shoulder, inhaling the scent of his cologne, barbecue, and the lingering scent of the bonfire. She smiled.

"Comfortable there?" Victor asked, his voice a rumble in his chest.

"Hmm," Jenny responded. She pulled reluctantly away from him and looked around them. Suddenly, her worries from earlier came crashing back. She yanked her hands away. "Sorry," she said, feeling a heavy blush creep up her cheeks.

"What are you sorry for, darling?" Victor asked, chuckling at her as he tried to get her hands back.

"Uh uh," Jenny said, shoving her hands into her pockets. She looked around. "Look, can we go somewhere and...talk? Maybe?" The realization that any of the other parents...or her coworkers...or anyone else in the town could see them was like a bucket of ice-water dumped over.

"Sure thing—come on." Victor took her arm, and although Jenny knew she should pull away, she couldn't find it in her to continue protesting. If this was the last human-to-human contact she was ever going to get from him, she wanted to enjoy it.

Surprisingly, she felt tears in her eyes at the thought that she was going to have to ruin this before they could even really get started. But there was nothing else for it.

"Where are we going?" Jenny asked as they continued walking even after they'd left the crowds of people behind.

"Shh," Victor said, smiling down at her. "Just wait. You'll see."

Suddenly, they veered to the right, off the main road and into the trees. Jenny had a wild moment of panic spurred by years of horror movies—was Victor taking her out into the woods to kill her? But no, he was a good guy, wasn't he?

"Relax," Victor said, a laugh in his tone. He tapped at her fingertips, which had tightened in a vice-like grip around his forearm. "Just wait."

They finally, after a lot of stumbling about in the near-blackness, came to a clearing. The moonlight shone down around them, illuminating a paddock full of horses.

Victor hopped up onto the paddock's fence and helped her up as well. "This is my upper pasture," he said. "We've got the horses up here for now while the weather's still okay; we'll move them closer to the house once the winter really sets in."

"Oh," Jenny said faintly. She shook her head. "I've never ridden a horse before."

"What?" Victor said, sounding appalled. "*Never?*"

"I mean, I rode one of those guided things at the zoo once, I guess," Jenny said. She shrugged. "I grew up in upstate New York. We weren't big on horses there. I mean, maybe I could have ridden a cow if I'd wanted to." She gave a soft laugh.

Victor shook his head. "We'll need to fix that," he said firmly. "Can't be a Texas cowgirl if you've never ridden a horse!"

"Who said anything about being a Texas cowgirl?" Jenny asked, laughing again. She pushed lightly at Victor's shoulder, and he put an arm around her, pulling her close.

"I know what we'll be doing all next summer when you're off from school," Victor said.

Jenny sighed and pulled slowly away. "Victor," she said, a warning note in her voice.

"There you go again," he said with a frown. "You're Mikey's teacher, and..."

"I like you!" Jenny blurted out. She blushed and clapped a hand over her mouth, unable to believe she had just said it like that, no tact at all.

Victor was laughing. "Oh darling. Well, I like you too—that's why I wanted to bring you to the festival tonight, so I could spend some more time with you."

Jenny shook her head. "No, Victor, I mean I–" She groaned and buried her face in her hands. "I mean I *like* you. You're incredibly handsome, and you're charming, and you're funny, and... And I can't. I'm Mikey's teacher; I can't...get involved with you."

There was a long silence in the clearing. On the opposite side of the pasture, one of the horses whinnied.

Finally, Victor sighed. "You're right, of course," he said. "In a town this small, everyone gossips like crazy. We've probably already rocked the boat a little tonight."

Jenny winced. "I can only hope everyone else was equally...out of character."

"Out of character?" Victor scoffed. "You looked like you were having the time of your life. If that's you out of character, then you need to get out more."

Jenny sighed. "It's not that easy. Especially not in a small town like this. I'm a teacher, Victor. I'm supposed to be someone the kids look up to. I'm not supposed to be someone who really exists outside of school—or else I compromise every ounce of respect they have for me." She frowned. "Not that I command any respect anyway," she muttered. "Mikey's seen to that."

"Hey now," Victor said, and Jenny could hear a hint of anger in his voice. "Mikey may not be the best kid at all times, but he's not the cause of all your problems in that class. And if you managed to discipline him properly, your problems would go away."

"Oh?" Jenny asked archly. "And how exactly should I be disciplining him? I've tried everything I can think of—and none of it seems to have an effect! If you didn't put up with his bratty behavior at home–" She cut herself off, chest heaving. "I'm sorry," she said quickly. "Victor, I'm sorry. That was out of line—I shouldn't have said that. Your home life is none of my business, and I–"

Victor hopped off the fence and started off through the pasture. "I'm going to call it a night," he said over his shoulder. "See you around."

"Wait!" Jenny cried, chasing after him. She caught his arm and yanked at it, forcing him to stop and turn to face her. She looked up at him through her eyelashes, and in the moonlight, Victor could see a couple tears clinging to her lashes. "Victor, I–" She gestured back at the darkness behind them. "First of all, I don't know where I'm going." She laughed, but Victor remained impassive. "And I'm sorry. You've been nothing but good to me since you met me, and I've been a real heel tonight. Just, this is my first job after college, and I...really don't want to mess it up. Especially since I came halfway across the country for it. Last thing I want is to go crawling home with my tail between my legs."

Victor sighed. "Come on. Your things are still in my truck anyway."

Chapter Four

Jenny didn't see Victor again for the next month and a half. Things were starting to settle down in her classroom—thanks in part to the fact that she'd been really strict on her homework assignments and tests and the students had begun to realize that they *had* to pay attention in class if they wanted to pass. She had required that their mid-term grades be signed by each of their parents, and that had been a rude awakening for a lot of the kids.

And that, she was sure, was why Victor was there in her classroom one afternoon in November, with no Mikey in sight.

He stood almost awkwardly in the doorway, where once he would have leaned comfortably, with an air of ease about him. "May I come in?" he asked.

Jenny inclined her head graciously. "Of course, Mr. Leonards. How can I help you today?"

"Actually, I was thinking that maybe I'd be able to help you," Victor said. "And please, you can be as frosty and unfamiliar as you'd like with me—but call me 'Victor'. 'Mr. Leonards' will always be my father."

"How are you planning to help me?" Jenny asked. "We have no field trips coming up."

"No, I know," Victor said. "But I also know you do have the bake sale coming up. Now, I'm not a great baker, but I was thinking that maybe you could hold the bake sale at my ranch instead of at the gym. Then, you could also sell horse rides to everyone who shows up. Brings in a little bit more money than a brownie does, and on my end, it would be great advertising for the ranch, if anyone's interested in lessons. We could do it for cheap, too—say, $5 and you can ride for five minutes, plus $0.50 for every minute after that. Cap it at ten minutes, but if you choose to take a real lesson, you'll get a discount of 50%. And half the proceeds of those lessons could go to the science wing as well."

Jenny frowned. "Sounds like *very* good advertising for you."

"But it's good for the bake sale too—I swear!" Victor said. "Look, you're living in cowboy country now, okay? I know *you* have never ridden a horse, but the kids here all *dream* of owning their own horse. Well, maybe not all of them, but many of them. They'll drag their parents along with them—it'll be like a carnival."

"We could make it like a carnival," Jenny said slowly, the gears turning in her head. "We could have some of those plywood boards with balloons on them and darts, and things like that." She frowned. "That could actually work."

"Just make sure the kids aren't throwing darts in the direction of the horses," Victor said with a laugh.

Jenny smiled at him, but then her smile faded. "But what reason do I give for holding it at *your* ranch?" she asked. "I'm sure some of the other parents own horses as well."

Victor raised an eyebrow at her. "Always over-complicating things," he muttered. Louder, he said, "Because it was my idea, maybe?"

Jenny laughed a little. "Well yeah, I suppose there is that." She shook her head. "All right. Consider it a deal. We'll need to start drawing up flyers and spreading the word... The PTA, we'll need to let the PTA know... And..."

"And you'll need to come over to my place for a ride," Victor said, grinning like the cat that had got the cream. "You know, to make sure everything's safe and that I'm not going to get one of the kids injured."

Jenny blinked at him and then shook her head. "I should've known you were up to something."

"What's a good day for you, Ms. Pritchard? Saturday?"

"Now, I'm not so sure," Jenny said. She shook her head. "Victor, if that's what you came here for—look, the idea sounded great, but–"

"Can't back out now, darling," Victor said, winking at her. "You already said it was a deal."

There was a long silence. "Saturday's fine," Jenny finally said faintly.

Victor grinned crookedly at her. "Saturday it is, then," he agreed. "Shall I pick you up or can you get there on your own?"

"I'll get there," Jenny said. She wanted to make sure she had an escape route if necessary.

"Wonderful," Victor said, tapping the brim of his hat. "I look forward to seeing you."

When he exited the room, Jenny slumped against the nearest desk, wondering just what she had just gotten herself into.

Chapter Five

"All right, that's it Keira—but remember, keep your heels down!" Victor called from the edge of the practice rink.

Jenny coughed lightly and waited for him to notice her. She smiled weakly in response to the man's brilliant smile. "Hey," she said. "I hope I'm not late."

"Right on time," Victor said, grinning at her. "Glad to see you. And you're looking mighty cute in that hat and those boots."

Jenny blushed and scuffed the toe of her boots across the floor. "Well, I figured if you were going to make me a cowgirl, I might as well at least look the part."

Victor tugged gently at one of her pigtails. "These are my favorite part—you're so adorable," he said, causing Jenny to blush an even deeper shade of red.

She shoved his hand away. "Yeah, yeah. So what am I supposed to do?"

"Just let me finish up with Keira and we'll get Shadow all saddled up for your first lesson," Victor said. "She's only got another five minutes on the clock, although it'll probably stretch to ten." He fondly watched the young rider in the rink.

Jenny hopped up on the fence. "How old is she?"

"Just fifteen. Real little devil, too—but good with the horses. She'll be in the Olympics one day, I swear."

"Hmm." Jenny watched the rest of the lesson, only sparing half a glance for the young girl in the rink. "You're a good coach," she said when the lesson was done.

Victor smiled over at her. "I've wanted to do this since I was a kid," he admitted. "Well, I mean, there was a time when I thought I'd be, I don't know, coaching football or baseball or something instead. But I always wanted to coach."

"Not to be the star?" Jenny asked curiously.

"Oh no," Victor said, shaking his head as he grabbed Keira's horse's reins. "I've always been much more comfortable in the background. And coaching is just as important as competing." He led Keira's horse back to the stables and held the animal still while the girl slid down to the ground. "Good job today, Keira," he praised. "Think you can get Myra cooled down all on your own?"

"Sure thing, Vic!" Keira chirped, taking the reins in her own small hand.

"Now," Victor said, rubbing his hands together, "let's get Shadow ready for you." He led Jenny to a stall at the back of the stables, where a tall black horse whickered at their arrival. Victor let them both into the stall and began affixing a bridle onto the horse. "Now I have to warn you, Shadow's a bit high-strung—and normally I wouldn't start a beginner on him, but I think the two of you will get along well."

"Oh really?" Jenny asked doubtfully.

"I think you can handle yourself," Victor said. He put a hand gently in the small of Jenny's back. "But if there's any point where you don't feel safe or comfortable..."

Jenny turned to look at him and was surprised to find their faces only inches apart in the tightness of the stall. If she just leaned in the barest amount, they'd be kissing...

She shuddered and pulled away, not that there was really anywhere to go.

Victor grinned and tugged her back out of the stall. Then, he led Shadow out as well. In short time, he had the horse all saddled up and ready to go, and then he turned back to Jenny. "Need a leg up?"

Jenny looked mistrustfully at the horse. "I'm not so sure this is a good idea..." she said uncertainly.

"You're right, hold on—just hold him right here," Victor said, passing the lead over to Jenny. He darted off down the aisle and returned a few minutes later with a helmet, which he plopped down on Jenny's head, doing up the buckle under her chin. "That's better," he said, nodding at her. "Safety first. Now..."

Jenny lightly touched the helmet and then turned towards the horse. She hesitantly stepped up to it's side and then lifted her leg up until she could put her toe in the stirrup. "Three—two—one," she muttered, squeezing her eyes shut as she pushed herself up and astride the horse.

"Oh wow, we have a natural here," Victor joked.

Jenny cracked her eyes open, scowling down at him. "Far from it," she said. "But what else was I supposed to do?"

Victor snorted. "Indeed. Come on." He led them out into the practice ring. "Now, this being your first lesson, I figure I'll be there with you every step of the way, all right? First, I'll just lead the two of you around at a walk. If you're feeling comfortable with that and think you can do better, maybe we'll take it into a trot—but I'm warning you, a trot may leave you feeling like a sack of potatoes being tossed around. It might be too much for your first lesson."

"I'll tell you when it's too much," Jenny said, tossing her head a little.

Victor grinned. "That's the spirit. Now, how do you feel up there right now?"

"I'm fine as long as it...stops moving," Jenny muttered, rubbing at the back of her neck.

Victor grinned. "Not enjoying it, then?" he asked.

"Where should I even be putting my hands?" Jenny asked, flapping her hands uselessly. "And is there something I should be...doing?"

"Your hands should be here, on the reins," Victor instructed, reaching up to help her place her hands. "See, pull back and he stops. Or let out some slack and he'll start walking. Or if he's being lazy and doesn't start walking, you can dig your heels into his sides a little." He unclipped the lead line. "I get the feeling you're just ready to do this on your own," he said. "And don't worry—some students are just like that. It's natural."

He watched her take a lap of the ring. "I'm going to go saddle up another horse," he told her when she had come around. "You keep doing easy circles, okay? And if anything happens and you don't want to do this anymore, you just get off his back and hop over the fence, okay? But you shouldn't have any problems."

"Okay," Jenny agreed. She shook her head. "This is easier than I thought it would be."

"You're doing great," Victor said. He jogged off to get a horse for himself.

When he got back into the rink, Jenny had Shadow trotting around the rink at a measured pace. "Are you sure you've never done this before?" he asked suspiciously, pulling Freya into a trot next to Shadow.

Jenny looked at him with wide eyes. "No!" she exclaimed. "Is this okay?"

"You're a natural," Victor said, shaking his head. He smiled at her. "It's a dangerous thing, Ms. Pritchard—all your charms, and you're a darned fine cowgirl to boot. What's a man to do?"

"Victor," Jenny sighed, slumping forwards. "Like I said before, we can't..."

"Because you're Mikey's teacher," Victor said.

"Because I'm Mikey's teacher," Jenny agreed.

"Is that the only reason?" Victor pressed.

"I mean... Well, yes," Jenny said. "But there's no getting around that one."

"Are you sure?" Victor asked, looking smug. He tugged at his reins, and Freya stopped easily. Shadow stopped as well, heeding his presence more than Jenny's hand on the reins.

"What do you mean?" Jenny asked, twisting in the saddle to face him.

"Cecile and I have been talking to Principal Mathers for a while now," Victor said. "And we've all agreed that for this year at least, it would be better if we homeschooled Mikey. Once he's settled in here, it'll be easier for him to make friends without being such a brat. And that gives him plenty of specialized attention like he needs. There will be a tutor coming by five days a week to work with him."

"You can't just pull him from school!" Jenny began, outraged on behalf of Mikey.

Victor laid a hand on her knee. "We asked him, Jenny. And it's what he wants to do."

"Oh." Jenny frowned, trying to process. "So in that case..."

"In that case, you're no longer Mikey's teacher," Victor finished. He gave Jenny a serious look. "So is that the only thing that kept you from allowing me to kiss you, *Ms. Pritchard*?"

Jenny giggled a little, shaking her head. "I suppose it was," she agreed, tilting her head in.

BITTERSWEET

KATE VALDEZ

Drizzle fell on her face as she got out of the café, pushing the glass doors open with trembling hands. Sandra Taylor let out a shaky breath while she pulled down the scarf covering the lower part of her face.

She stood still for a moment and after gathering her composure back, she walked to a random direction, fished out the crumpled paper in her pocket, and dropped it unceremoniously in the nearest trash bin. People walked past her without a glance, but she felt like she was being watched, that they knew and were secretly judging her.

She knew she did the right thing. He clearly disregarded his promise as if Sandra's feelings didn't matter. She was only taking vengeance and justice in her own way.

She was fed up. And he deserveD to die.

***

The moonlight seeped past the floral curtains hanging in her windows, casting a faint glow on her bed. It's late but Sandra kept on turning, kicking off her blankets and pulling it up again. Faint sounds of cars speeding by did nothing to distract her from her thoughts, her ash brown hair spread on her pillows messily as she stared at the white ceiling.

The thought of what was about to happen in the coming days caused an unsettling feeling but at the back of her mind, she believes that Aiden committed a mistake worth his life. Despite everything, they shared for the past years and the guilt and doubt filling her heart, she was certain of her decision.

If only he did not cheat on her. If he did not broke his promise that he swore to always keep, then Sandra would not have done this.

The thought of Aiden with another girl the other day drove her insane and summoned the devils in her mind. It cornered her to an idea that was long ago put on the back burner but suddenly sounded appealing that moment. She thought about it for days, but no matter how she fought with the rational part of her mind, the pain brought about by her ex-boyfriend cannot be erased.

The first time it happened was a year ago. Aiden cheated on her with a rookie model he worked with. He dated her and bought her things, and made up excuses to Sandra that he was too busy and she completely fell for them. It went on for months and Sandra didn't have a clue until one of her friends saw them together in a mall which was a bit far from the busy parts of the city, the areas where Sandra rarely went to.

It was devastating and humiliating.

When she confronted him, the fight that ensued was unimaginably nasty. Insults and swears were thrown at each other like daggers while petty faults and promises were dug up and created a bigger mess. In the end, when they both lost their steam, Aiden apologized and promised to never cheat again, which Sandra held on to like sacred words. She loves him and even if he had hurt her, she chose to believe in his words.

The past year was promising. Feelings blossomed after the hurdle and their relationship had developed to a point where Sandra thought that it wouldn't be long before they decided to tie the knot.

They never discussed a wedding nor their lives together in the far future but she was hopeful that Aiden was feeling the same. They have changed for the better and learned the ropes and dynamics of their relationship, knew which things tick off the other and which ones make them happy.

With her successful career as a magazine editor and a blissful relationship with Aiden, Sandra felt that everything couldn't be better. Or so she thought until she witnessed him the other day enter a hotel with a girl.

She may have easily dismissed it as a client or model for a photo shoot since it was a classy hotel often used for pictorials. As a photographer, Aiden has worked with countless models and celebrities and it was never an issue for her. But that day, it was just the two of them dressed in casual clothes, walking side by side while talking animatedly, unaware that Sandra was only a few feet away, watching them with unbelieving eyes.

She was tempted to come up to them and cause a scene but the sight made her knees weak and tremble. She turned away before breaking down in public and opted to pour out her anguish inside her car.

They were supposed to meet later that day but she did not show up, breaking up with him through a phone call. He kept on asking her why but she hung up, turned off her phone, and blocked his e-mail for good measure. The recurring memory of that moment haunted Sandra over and over again and anger, jealousy, and spite clouded her mind and encouraged irrational thoughts.

She heaved a deep sigh and continued to stare at the white. It was completely silent for a moment, with no sound of car honks and cahoots from outside her room. Bringing a hand to her hair, she tugged at it and balled her hands into fists before she turned around and buried her face in her pillow. The cushion muffled her screams and sobs. It was soaked in tears in no time while she cried her eyes out.

This will end in a few days. All she had to do was to wait.

***

Bag hanging in one hand and the other busy with her phone, she strolled through their office, pausing from time to time to greet the staff good morning. The sound of ringing phones and jammed photocopying machines felt familiar, just the typical scenarios that greet the start of her day.

She went straight for the far left corner where her private cubicle is, only to stop when she spotted a small vase filled with flowers sitting on her desk. A bunch of lilacs and white petals were in it, tightly wounded together by a pink ribbon to and created a beautiful arrangement.

A man cleared his throat behind her and she closed her eyes, recognizing the voice even if he has not yet said anything.

She went straight to her chair and dropped her bag. "What do you need?" she asked coldly without facing him.

"I want to know why you broke up with me. It's been days and you did a great job evading my calls and messages," Aiden MacNeil sighed and took a step closer.

The editor scoffed and faced him. "You're actually asking me that?"

He looked at her with a puzzled expression. "Of course, I am!" He hissed, mindful of the other people who are probably straining their ears to hear their conversation.

He lowered his voice back to normal. "We scheduled to meet that day but you stood me up without any warning and when you finally picked up your phone, you just said that you were breaking up with me and hung up. You didn't even wait for my response."

"What for? To hear your excuses? I'm not falling for your lies again, Aiden. We're over. Now please leave. I have work to do," she gestured at the pile of papers on her desk and glared at him.

Aiden went closer until he was an arm away. "I honestly don't know what you are talking about," he said determinedly, meeting her eye to eye.

"I saw you that day," she declared, shoulders tensed and fists clenched. "You were with a girl and you entered a hotel. That wasn't for work Aiden, I'm sure of it."

Surprised, Aiden dragged a hand down his face exasperatedly.

"Okay, listen." Sandra attempted to get out but he was faster, blocking her way with an arm. "Why did we arrange to meet up during that day?" He paused. "Because that day was our fourth anniversary," he continued when he didn't receive a response.

Putting his hands on her shoulders to motion her to take a seat, he continued his explanation. "It's true. I was with a girl. She was a friend of mine back in college but we didn't really keep in touch that's why you've never met her."

"She was there to help me." He licked his lips, a nervous habit. "I was planning something for you and she offered her help. I got a room in the hotel and that time when you saw us, we went there early to finish it on time before we met." He admitted.

Sandra remained quiet, assessing his story and expression. She had come to learn Aiden to the point that she knows when he is lying. And this time, he is not. There was that sincerity in his eyes, unwavering under her scrutinizing glare.

"She was only there to help? Nothing more?" She asked, testing if Aiden would even blink, stutter, or avoid her eyes.

He pulled the phone from his front pocket. "I can call her now and you may speak to her directly if you want to," he offered, handing her the phone which showed that he is indeed calling a girl.

Alarmed, the editor snatched the phone and ended the call before it even connected. Nothing in his explanation seemed amiss. If he was indeed cheating, he'd never risk getting caught by bringing the other girl somewhere near their meeting place.

Dread crept up to Sandra and she reached for her bag. "What have I done," she muttered nervously as she rummaged her bag for her phone and scrolled her call logs, only to find all entries erased until she realized that she deleted everything yesterday after her meeting with him.

Stooping down to meet her on eye level, Aiden lifted her face with a finger beneath her chin. "Do you believe me now?" He asked despite being puzzled with her weird behavior.

He only received frantic nods as a response before Sandra resumed pulling everything she had in her bag, browsing the papers and notebooks particularly.

"Hey, what's wrong? What are you looking for?"

Sandra looked at him with horrified eyes. "His number, I need his contact number. I need to tell him to stop, that I'm canceling everything."

"What are you talking about? Calm down and tell me what's happening," he coaxed, alarmed at the fear in her eyes.

She looked around before leading him out of her office. They walked along the hallways without a word and Sandra led him to the barely-used staircase.

When they arrived, she closed the door carefully and let go of his hand.

She gnawed on her lower lip, the flesh turning reddish pink with the repeated pressure. "I made a big mistake. Please promise you won't run away if I tell you."

Aiden nodded, suddenly nervous at where this conversation is going.

"I hired a hitman."

Silence rung in the area while Aiden waited for her to continue, expecting a giggle, a scoff, or anything that would tell him that she was just joking—that she was just playing with him. With the way she said it and how she was acting, he feared that she was implying that she hired a hitman to kill him, her boyfriend.

Hearing nothing else from her for a minute, he blanched. "Why?" he almost whispered.

He was beyond shocked. Who wouldn't be if they knew that the person they were in a relationship with just paid someone to kill them. It caused more than just an unsettling feeling and he can feel the start of nausea.

The editor started walking back and forth, from one wall to the other, avoiding his eyes. "I was frustrated! Angry, devastated and scandalized. I thought you were cheating on me again and I felt used and stupid. Every part of me was screaming to get back at you, to avenge in any way so I can give you as much pain that you caused me."

"But getting me killed?" he shouted, unable to believe what he was hearing.

"I was desperate Aiden! I see red whenever I recall you with that girl. I wasn't able to think rationally!" she argued, but her voice was wavering.

"But what about now that you know the truth? Do you still want me to be dead?" he asked in a sarcastic tone. "I came here to make amends with you, only to know that you paid someone out there to kill me. This is outrageous Sandra! You didn't even try to hear me out," he shouted. There was a tremor in his voice and Sandra cannot blame him. He had every right to be angry.

"I know and I'm sorry! I was blinded by everything. I'll try to contact him, tell him that everything we talked about should be forgotten."

She was convinced that she never had to communicate with him again because their agreement was simple. The hitman had to kill the person as instructed and she had to pay him the agreed amount—that was all. She never thought something like this would happen.

Aiden paced while waving his hands frantically. "Then tell him right away! Who knows, I might drop dead the moment I get out of this building!"

Sandra shuddered at the image.

"I can't." She admitted, looking at him with worry. "I discarded his contacts, I don't have his number anymore." She looked at him pleadingly, trying to convince him that she was regretting her decision.

Aiden brought a hand to his forehead and massaged his temple. "Where did you even got his number?"

Sandra's eyes brightened at the question and she ran back to her office, the photographer in tow, and scrolled through her contacts.

"Ethan, I need his number again. I lost it," she said when the said man picked up, not bothering to say hello.

Startled by the sound of her voice, he responded with an okay and promised to call back immediately. Meanwhile, Aiden pursed his lips when he knew who his girlfriend's source was. Of course, it was him, the bitter ex. He was tempted to confront her now but it was not the right time.

Sandra drummed her fingers on the table as they waited. Aiden remained standing beside her and stared at her phone intently. They both jumped in surprise when it rang.

"I can't contact him anymore."

"What do you mean? You were the one who gave me his contacts just a few days ago!"

"I'll only know of his new number after a few days. The one who has direct contact with him told me that he often changed his numbers and usually took a few days before he informed people. I tried calling the number I have but I wasn't able to connect." He explained. "What's wrong Sandra? Didn't you tell me you'll only meet him once? I assume you've already met yesterday. Did something happen?"

Sandra bit her lip to fight back a sob. "Change of plans. I don't want to do it anymore," she glanced at Aiden who tensed at her words.

Ethan stayed silent for a moment. "I'm sorry," he apologized in a low voice, obviously not expecting to hear that. "I can't do anything about that right now but I promise to let you know once I get a hold of him again," he hung up afterward after promising Sandra that he will call as soon as he can.

Aiden swallowed a lump in his throat. "What now?" His face was pale and beads of sweat were forming on his forehead. Sandra wrapped her arms around him, biting back a sob. "I'm so sorry."

***

They decided to take the day off from work and drove back to Aiden's apartment using Sandra's car. They have no idea if the hitman would trail after Aiden's car so they tried to be safe.

With a shaky voice, the editor relayed how her meeting with the hitman went, while Aiden listened and tried hard to focus on the road. Sandra told him that she never gave details on how it should be done. All she provided were Aiden's pictures and usual daily schedule. Even the exact day nor time, she had no clue as to when the hitman will strike. Aiden tightened his grip on the steering wheel upon the information.

The drive back was uneventful which they were both thankful for. Sandra's nerves were on the high and she kept on glancing out the windows, checking if there was someone who may look familiar among the sea of strangers.

She rubbed her face with a hand in frustration. That was another problem. She never saw his face clearly.

When she met him the other day, she only informed him of what she was wearing. Afraid that someone would have recognized her talking to him, she covered almost half of her face with a scarf. He only approached her and sat beside her among the row of seats before she slid the envelope containing the pictures, details, and the money to him. When he gave a signal that he was okay with it, Sandra went out immediately and only saw him in her periphery.

They made it to Aiden's building and took the elevator without exchanging any words. Sandra bit her lower lip and looked at him pleadingly, hoping to hear anything but the silence echoed loud in her ears.

The editor followed Aiden as he walked on the hallways where his unit is. Still a bit out of his senses with the recent revelations, he pushed the door open and walked in, tensing when he suddenly felt weird.

He eyed the sliding door to his balcony, thinking if he had really left the door open despite not using it for weeks now. Alarmed, he ran over to Sandra and forced her to crouch down on the floor.

"What? What happened? Is there anyone here?" The hysterical female asked, peeking at the balcony from where she laid flat on the floor.

"I don't know. But I'm sure I didn't leave that door open when I left earlier," he whispered back, straining his ears to make sure there were no other noises coming from the rooms.

He beckoned Sandra to the door, all the while maintaining his arm protectively wrapped around her waist. They crawled all the way and breathed a sigh of relief when they make it out unharmed.

Aiden leaned on the wall and pulled her beside him, enveloping her shaking hands with his as he tried to coax her to calm down.

"It might be a false alarm," he tried to say it in a steady voice but failed miserably, the slight stutter giving away how nervous he was as well.

Sandra shook her head no and swallowed a lump in her throat. "It may not be. He knows where you live Aiden," she looked at him with remorse and regret.

"We should get going then," he pulled her up, ignoring the pang in his heart, and almost sprinted towards the elevator, holding her hand tightly as he thought of a plan to get out of this mess.

***

They decided to drive out of the city and stay in a room at the outskirts. Sandra kept on looking outside their room to check for any suspicious man, but her efforts turned out futile. Somehow, it made her feel relieved too.

She reclined on the bed's headboard and banged her head on the wood, causing Aiden to look up from the floor where he was seated.

He approached her and held her hand. "Hey, it's alright. We'll get out of this."

"But how?" she is too tempted to cry by this time. The gravity of what she had done was just sinking in and nausea crept at her insides, making her stomach churn unpleasantly.

"Can you try calling Ethan again?" he gestured at her phone which she had been holding on to for dear life during the whole drive.

She obliged and dialed the male's number, only to receive a voice mail. "His phone's off," she frowned, confused.

Aiden huffed upon seeing her expression and paced back and forth across the room. "We have to be somewhere safe. But where?" he muttered to himself. Sandra watched him helplessly. She wanted to help, but she didn't know how.

Seeking the help of the police is an option but it means she might be in trouble. After all, she is the main perpetrator and none of these would have happened if she just took the time to listen to her boyfriend.

"Aiden," she called weakly. "Maybe I should go back. I'll try to find him myself and ask around. This was my fault so I should solve it myself." She stood up from the bed and went straight to the door only to be halted by Aiden.

His grip around her arm was tight and Sandra forced herself not to wince in pain. "No, we'll do it together. I can't let you do it alone. It's dangerous."

"But I'm not in danger, you are. He won't harm me. I was the one who paid him," she regretted the words as soon as they came out from her mouth. The photographer's eyes twitched upon being reminded that the girl in front of him was the one who ordered his death.

Nonetheless, he pulled her towards him and wrapped his arms around her, resting a hand on her head as he muttered words of encouragement.

"We'll do this. Together, alright?" he looked down at her to meet her eyes which were shining with unshed tears. Though hesitant, she nodded.

***

The next day was another fruitless attempt to get a hold of Ethan and Sandra was growing impatient. Ethan knew how serious and dangerous their situation was so she cannot fathom why she can't contact him now of all instances.

They decided to come back to the city to test their luck. If they cannot stop the hitman through other people, they might as well take the chance to see him directly. It was a big risk, but at this moment, they were willing to do anything.

Fortunately, the windows of Sandra's car were tainted, offering some sort of protection. They drove along the city's streets slowly, going to places where Aiden frequented, particularly those that Sandra had specified to the hitman.

They stayed outside his apartment's building for about an hour but failed to see anyone suspicious. They also checked his workplace until the end of working hours but had no progress. Either the man was nowhere near the vicinity or that he's really an expert when it comes to blending in with the crowd.

By the end of the day, they both remained quiet as they drove back, mentally and physically exhausted.

***

Sandra lay on her side, away from Aiden. The tears were threatening to fall since they were on their drive back but she held on, not wanting the photographer to see her in that state.

She muffled her sobs, covering her mouth with a hand while the tears streamed down her face. She glanced back at Aiden, who has fallen asleep almost instantly, tired from driving for a whole day.

'How could he still tolerate seeing me? He must hate me now.' She wondered, tracing his facial features with her eyes and committing them to memory. Once this has settled down, she won't be surprised if he decides to run away from her. By now, she didn't even know if they are still together. Any sane person would hate someone like her.

Forcing her eyes to close, Sandra wished she had taken at least one good look at the man she hired as a hitman. If only she did then they would at least have a clue to who they are against with.

A flash of black lines crossed her vision and her eyes snapped open and widened in surprise.

The man has a black mark on his right hand. It may be a birthmark or a tattoo but she was sure that it was there. She looked at Aiden, suddenly ecstatic for remembering something, and the urge to tell him was strong. But one look at him and she forced the excitement down.

She slept that night with more hope that tomorrow will not be another failure.

***

The drive back to the city was quiet again and Aiden kept glancing at Sandra, trying to read what was on her mind. She has not spoken a word since they woke up and he was starting to worry.

He stretched his hand and covered hers which was rested on her lap. He caressed the hand with his thumb and smiled at her briefly, which she returned. "Anything wrong?"

Shaking her head, she went back to looking outside the car and the photographer inwardly sighed.

"Tell me what's on your mind."

She was silent for a moment before giving in. "I was wondering how can you still talk to me and not be horrified or disgusted," she finally answered truthfully. She just had to let him know to keep her sanity intact.

Aiden almost stepped on the brakes but stopped himself from doing so and opted to just slow down instead.

Stealing a glance, he saw her blank expression from the reflection in the glass window. "I'm not disgusted at you, Sandra. I'll never be. Why would you even think that?"

The editor shrugged nonchalantly. "That should be the logical reaction, right? I mean, we're in danger because of m—," he cut off her sentence abruptly.

"Stop saying that. It was probably a wrong decision but you should not blame yourself. Your judgment was clouded because of your emotions," he defended. His voice was sharp and it was obvious that he won't hear anything more about it.

Sandra almost cried. Despite everything, Aiden was defending her against herself.

She kept her mouth shut the rest of the ride, not wanting to argue further.

***

They were outside Aiden's workplace again when his phone rang.

He looked at her before answering. "Yes, speaking," he replied. "No, sorry. I forgot to call in sick. I won't be able to go in today as well," he sighed heavily. "I'm sorry. I'm...resting. I'll be back as soon as I can," he hung up and threw his phone on the dashboard.

Sandra lowered her head, guilt and shame flooding her once again.

"I'll go get us some snacks," he said before climbing out of the car and going straight to the café across the road. She tried to tell him to stop because it might not be safe but he was already out and crossing the street before she processed everything. She can only look at his back longingly.

A few minutes later, he was out of the café carrying a brown paper bag in one hand and a holder carrying two cups of coffee on the other. The lights turned green and he began to cross the street. All the while, Sandra fixed her eyes on him when suddenly; she heard the loud screeching of tires nearing.

Aiden was one among the few pedestrians who were behind the large throng of people crossing. The black car suddenly came out of nowhere and sped through the other idle cars in the street, moving so fast and going directly at the pedestrian lane.

Some people screamed and watched in horror as the car came near, while the others scrambled far from it. Aiden, belatedly realizing what was happening, jumped out of its way just in time. Any second later and he would've been hit badly.

The paper bag and cups of coffee were spilled on the ground and he stood up angrily and marched towards the car which stopped inches away from the streetlight.

Angered, he knocked on the window twice but received no response. "Hey, come out! Are you crazy?"

The door to the driver's seat opened and out came a man, wearing a black shirt, black cap, and black pants. His head was lowered so Aiden cannot see his face clearly. He was about to confront him when a loud honk resounded and he snapped up, alarmed, and looked towards where they were parked.

The honk was coming from Sandra's car, unstopping, and the people nearby were starting to cover their ears. He stood there for a second, confused as to what was happening when it hit him.

He faced the man again, who was now pulling something from his back.

Aiden ran for the car, pushing other people out of his way, and zigzagged through the path to confuse him. The loud sound of a gunshot resounded causing the people to run away and cower in fear. Cars sped by, ignoring the traffic rules in favor of getting as far away as they can from the man who was holding a gun.

Another gunshot and Aiden's knees buckled in fear that he almost fell. He braced his hand on his knee and forced himself to run.

He was just a few steps away when pain pierced through his shoulder and something hard hit him. His eyes widened in shock and he almost stopped but the noise from Sandra's car was unrelenting and has now turned into frantic beeps.

He slid in the passenger door as soon as he was close enough and Sandra stepped on the engine as hard as she can, while she glanced at the side mirrors to check. The man was still shooting fearlessly before he climbed back to his car.

"Shit, he's going after us," she stepped on the breaks and turned left on a sharp curve, earning the angry honks of cars. She heard a groan and she turned to Aiden who was now clutching his bleeding shoulder.

"Oh, my god. You were shot!" she exclaimed. In her lost state earlier, she didn't even notice that the hitman managed to hurt him.

"Eyes on the road," Aiden warned through gritted teeth. He bit his lower lip hard until it bled to prevent himself from voicing his pain.

The editor obliged and drove through random streets, constantly checking if the black car was still following them. Her eyes flew to the male from time to time, grimacing when she saw the amount of blood on the car seat.

After a few more minutes when she deemed that they were safe, the black car nowhere in sight, Sandra went straight to the hospital, driving through random streets just to be sure.

The nurses immediately attended to Aiden when they arrived and she was relieved when she knew that the bullet wound seemed to be far from anywhere critical. His shoulder was still bleeding but his pained groans were reduced to heavy breaths and he has already stopped wincing in pain from time to time.

It took a few hours before he was transferred to a room. Sandra thanked the heavens that he's alright, that he's still alive. She cannot imagine how would she be right now if the hitman managed to kill him on the spot. She would never forgive herself.

He looked peaceful while he slept, his breaths even and calm. Sandra brushed away the hair strands that fell on his forehead and traced her hand down his nose, relishing the fact that he was still breathing. With his unguarded expression, she noticed the dark bags under his eyes and frowned, displeased that Aiden was never able to properly rest since the other day.

His shoulder was bandaged but the doctors already declared him stable and safe, though he has to stay a few more days to assure that the bullet wound would not be infected or reopen.

Licking her lips in thought, she stared blankly on the hospital bed's white sheets. Earlier, the sight of that man's hand shook her to the core and she was almost rooted on her seat. If not for the sudden adrenaline rush and the desire to save Aiden, she may not have warned him early enough.

She may have only seen that mark on his hand once but the man earlier just gave her the same aura—cold, unforgiving, carefree, and ruthless. She remembered how much she felt gooseflesh rising on her skin when they first met even though they didn't speak directly with each other.

Seeing how the hitman fired one bullet to another aimed at Aiden caused a shiver run down her spine. She wanted to help but she didn't have a clue how. She was helpless against a bullet and she definitely can't take him physically face to face, so she opted for the third logical option—which was to run as fast as they can. She was confident that they are safe in the hospital. She managed to lose him and she hoped that it take time before he found them again.

Clutching the cup of coffee with her chilly hands, she made her way to Aiden's room, determined to stay awake for the remainder of the night. It had been a day since he was confined and he was asleep most of the time, waking up for a few hours to eat, clean up, and comply with his check-ups and changing of bandage.

It was nearing midnight yet Sandra willed the sleep to go away. She had not slept a wink since they came here and now, her body was almost begging her to get some rest. The initial fear and shock were enough to keep her eyes open yesterday, but now she wanted to get even an ounce of sleep.

The television served as white noise as she fiddled with her phone. She has received at least a dozen calls and messages from people at work, asking her if she'll be on leave or if she was all right. Taking a leave for two consecutive days was already uncharacteristic of her. No wonder people began to worry.

Restless, she tried to call Ethan multiple times the whole day but he was out of reach. Sandra has resigned to the fact that he may not want to be involved in this affair, which was not surprising.

Her eyelids fluttered and she took a sip of her now cold coffee. She pinched her arm but to no avail, her vision began to blur with sleepiness. Eventually, Sandra surrendered to dreamland.

The sound of the door clicking disturbed Sandra's rest but she chose to keep her eyes closed, assuming that it was the nurse who comes during the wee hours of the day to check up on Aiden's vitals.

The other person's feet shuffled, soft steps against the tiled floor, and she could feel the person stopping beside her chair, which was close to Aiden's bed. She was tempted to continue her slumber but something bothered her, and she forced an eye to crack open just to check.

It was indeed the nurse, who was now leaning towards Aiden, blocking Sandra's view. The male nurse was probably checking the photographer's vitals but something bothered Sandra. There seems to be something off with the way the other person was acting that she cannot pinpoint.

Slowly, and as quietly as she could, she sat straight on her seat and stared at the nurse's back. She looked at the bedside drawer but saw no clipboards, which the nurses usually use when they do their rounds. His movements were quick but lacked the usual finesse of licensed professionals.

The editor gulped at the clawing fear inside her, hoping that she was wrong, that she was just being paranoid and there was no reason to be nervous.

She watched as the nurse lifted Aiden's head off the pillows and pulled the material away, clutching it with his large hands. Startled, her mouth opened in a silent scream upon seeing the nurse's hand, and she only managed to let out a gasp when the man whipped the pillow towards her direction, hitting her square on the face.

It brought Sandra tumbling down the floor, her chair falling causing a loud crashing sound which disturbed the silence of the night.

The man turned to her and his eyes were bloodshot, either he lacked sleep or he's on something.

Body trembling in fear, she pushed herself backward, sliding against the floor as she created as much distance between them as she could.

The hitman clicked his tongue and his mouth formed into a smug. Sandra watched horrified as the man took unhurried steps towards her and she continued to back away until she hit the corner.

The man continued to smirk. His clothes were white, almost identical to the nurses' uniform. But his face was morphed into a cold-blooded murderer who was about to kill them.

Sandra flinched when he was just a step away and for a second, she felt like screaming, but fear bit her tongue that she can only let out a whimper. He grabbed her nape harshly, his face close to hers and his warm, stinky breath blowing on her face.

He tugged at her hair and she screamed in pain, only to be hushed by the man's palm covering her mouth. "You were probably his other lady aren't you?" he smiled evilly, enjoying the sight of her with tears running down her face.

The editor shook her head no. She wanted to push him away and explain that he got it wrong, that she was the one who hired him in the first place. Her limbs felt numb and her whole body was shaking until it tensed at the feeling of a cold circular metal against her temple.

She whimpered and tried to pull away but he kept her in place, kicking her in the stomach when she attempted to kick him in the chest. Sandra groaned at the pain and she curled up into a ball, feeling her breath knocked out of her.

"I don't have time for this. You should've just run away, you know? I gave you a day, but you're still with him," he snickered and tugged her arm to make her stand. Her knees were wobbly and she struggled to remain upright. "Now I have no choice but to kill you as well."

Tears continued to cascade down her face, her eyes red and brimming. She wailed when he pushed her face against the wall and hissed when her head hit hard against the concrete. She gritted her teeth to ebb the pain away but it didn't subside.

The hospital hallways were quiet and Sandra's wishing that someone, anyone, will accidentally pass by and hear the commotion.

The editor inhaled a sharp breath when she felt that the barrel was pointed at her head again, just a little above her nape. She braced herself for the deafening shot, for the piercing sensation, but yelped in surprise when the man fell down on his knees, back arched.

Aiden was holding a chair, the one where Sandra was sat on. From his enraged expression and the hitman's reaction, he probably hit him hard with the chair on his back.

Sandra ran and hid behind him, clutching his hospital gown tightly. Aiden held on the chair tightly.

It didn't take long before the hitman was charging against them, grabbing Aiden's head like he was holding a doll, before punching him in the face. The photographer let go of his unconventional weapon at the impact.

"Stop!" Sandra screamed, slapping the man uselessly and earning his attention. The hit was too painful and she winced when his hand went straight to her face. It wounded her and she could feel the trickle of blood on the corner of her mouth.

With short breaths and a panicked, almost scratchy voice, she screamed again and struggled against his hold. A bunch of her hair was pulled and her scalp felt like it's burning with the exertion. She thrashed and kicked in the air but her efforts proved to be futile.

Aiden kicked the hitman's gun away which fell when he attacked Sandra. He aimed at the guy's crotch, kicking him hard before grabbing his hair in retaliation. The other guy is bigger than him, towering and muscular, and he barely reached his nose, but he cannot stand seeing him hurting his girlfriend.

The man elbowed Aiden and released Sandra, who fell in on the floor, heaving. Enraged, the man hit Aiden repeatedly and the smaller male can only use his arms to shield his body, his bullet wounds reopening with the assault.

Sandra watched the scene in horror and crawled towards the door, opened it and shouted for help. She screamed as loud as she can before running back to help Aiden, who was covered with bruises and blood.

Sandra could not stop crying and she hit the man as hard as she could with the pillow, the nearest thing she could reach. She screamed for him to stop, that she doesn't want Aiden to be killed anymore, but the man has turned deaf and tuned out everything around him. He was possessed with anger and the desire to kill the man beneath him, who has escaped his grasps multiple times in the past days.

Not giving up, Sandra run to the chair and raised it, ready to hit the man, only to be flung away with his arm yet again. Her lithe figure was no match for his strength and her whole body felt bruised and blue all over.

A glint beneath the bed caught her attention, which was the gun that Aiden kicked away earlier. The black deadly weapon stood out from the white floor and she didn't hesitate to crawl beneath the bed and retrieve it.

The metal felt cold and heavy in her grasp. She clutched it to her chest and she watched the fight helplessly, with Aiden lying on the floor motionlessly and the man continuing to rain punches down the other male's face and body. The only indication that Aiden was still conscious was his whimpers.

The man straddled him and landed another hit on his face, laughing loudly and clearly enjoying how he brought pain to Aiden, who knocked his head on the floor, the resounding crack reaching Sandra's ears. It looked like the man has almost forgotten about her, his focus entirely on Aiden beneath him.

Sandra took a few steps away and extended her hands, holding the gun with both of her hands. Her index finger was poised on the trigger and she aimed. She can feel the metal slide against her sweaty palms and she licked her chapped lips as she swallowed a large lump in her throat.

No one's dying between her and Aiden, so there was only one choice.

The sound of a gunshot disturbed the tranquil of the night. Sandra ended up on her knees, eyes dazed as blood pooled on the floor.

She rubbed her palms down her pants repeatedly until she can feel the skin burning. A larger hand took hers and she smiled at the owner, beyond relieved that apart from the bruises and his bullet wound reopening, Aiden did not suffer from other injuries.

The photographer tightened his grip on her hand before repeating his answer. "I am sure, Sir. I have no idea who may have wanted me to be killed. I have no enemies I am aware of," he met the direct stare of the officer, who has been trying to squeeze out any information about the case.

The police arrived almost a minute after Sandra shot the hitman dead. Apparently, the police have been tracking him down since the ruckus he has caused the other day.

The officer cleared his throat. "That man was one of the people on our most wanted list. We've been hunting him down ever since his first murder years ago. It's a known fact that he's a skilled hitman. We haven't seen any connections between you and him. The only possible link we saw on why he tried to kill you was because he was hired."

Aiden shook his head no while Sandra looked down, not uttering any words. "Or it could be that he was not in his right mind. I can't think of any reason why someone would want me dead..." the editor curled her toes at the words, "but I'm willing to cooperate with the investigation in any way I can," Aiden offered.

The officer sighed in resignation and bade them goodbye but not without reminding them that they will still be called for their official statements.

"You should have just told him the truth," Sandra muttered once they were alone again in the hospital room. Her face was pale yet her lips were bleeding. She looked like a mess.

"I deserved to be jailed for what I have done," she retrieved her hand from his and rested them on her lap.

"It was self-defence, Sandra. You weren't at fault," he reasoned.

"That's not what I was talking about," she snapped, frustrated that he chose to ignore the glaring truth in this case.

"I know," he affirmed. "But how many times do I have to tell you that I understand you and why you did it? I've long forgiven you," he put a hand on her knee and caressed the bluing bruise in there, softly tracing its edges with his finger.

Sandra sniffed and she started to cry again, covering her face with her hands in shame. "I don't deserve your forgiveness," she wailed, her breath hitching every now and then.

The photographer looked at her with worry in his eyes. He did not know what to do in order to convince her that she should forgive herself the same way he did. There was no point in dwelling on the mistakes born out of wrong assumptions and past wrongdoings. Aiden has accepted the fact that it was partly his fault. If he never gave her the reason to suspect and doubt him, then she would never have acted this way.

He pulled her against him and settled her on his lap. The position was a bit uncomfortable but the small couch was better than the hospital bed. He rested her head on his chest and tucked his chin on her forehead, caressing her back with his good hand.

He shushed her and rubbed comforting circles on her back. They stayed like that for a few minutes until her crying stopped and there was comfortable silence.

He contemplated on what to say but he had run out of words.

Instead, he braced himself for the long-delayed question. There could be no worse timing than now but he had to say it or he will chicken out again.

"Sandra," he began, breathing deeply when she responded with a hum while she cuddled closer to him. "Will you marry me?"

She jerked on his lap and looked at him with wide eyes, beyond shocked with his question.

"W-what—"

He smiled nervously. "It was the plan the other day. That time when you saw me," he flinched at the memory but continued with his explanation. "I was planning to propose but...well, things just didn't turn out the way I planned," he pursed his lips into a thin line, trying to read her expression.

"So now I'm taking this chance to ask you, will you be with me for the rest of our lives?"

Sandra, unable to express herself through words, pulled him carefully into a tight hug, remembering about his injured shoulder at the last minute. She cried again, this time because of happiness.

"I'll take that as a yes, then."

END

RESCUING REBECCA

GRETA GORHAM

It had not been that long ago that Rebecca had wondered why Sara wanted to hear the same bedtime stories again and again. Her daughter, so bright and vibrant and imaginative, surely needed more stimulation than the endless repetition of tales she already knew the end to. But, for all the ways Sara was unpredictable and unique in day to day life, frustrating her teachers and marvelling the elders, in this her daughter was as set in her ways as the frailest grandmother. Rebecca had tried to pretend the fable about the hare and the tortoise didn't bore her, tried to infuse every nightly telling with the same excitement, but at a certain point she had to admit she dreaded them. Once she managed to convince Hans to do it, but Sara swiftly sent her father out of the room. It just wasn't the same, and the same was what she wanted.

But, Rebecca supposed, circumstances could change anything, make the fondest things sour and the dullest things sweet. And now, a year after Hans' accident, a year since widowhood turned every sight that brought back every youthful memory ugly, Rebecca found that insipid fable had become, absurdly, something to hold on to.

Maybe in this was Sara was wise, she thought, as her daughter wriggled below the blankets and Rebecca adjusted them before blowing out the candle. The young seemed to adore unpredictability and once Rebecca had too. She had been considered wild and impetuous, warned again and again that she would never find a husband. She bored easily. Yet when your world was turned upside down and nothing remained where you left it, returning to the recognisable was really not so bad. In that way, Sara had proved herself so much cleverer than her parents ever were. In the days, play and exploration and adventure, a new thing to discover around every corner. By night, the warmth of home and the knowledge that the tortoise would always beat that smug hare. Boredom became comfort and comfort was best shared when you both lost something.

Placing the book on Sara's bedside table (she wondered why she even bothered with it anymore; she knew the words by heart) Rebecca walked out into the hall of her modest house and turned the corner into the kitchen. Flames crackled in the fireplace and the warm smell of dinner still lingered as candles bathed everything in a gentle orange light. Rebecca took it all in and, as she did every night, searched for that old feeling of contentedness at the beautiful home that was hers.

That was a routine she would sooner give up.

She sat at the table and closed her eyes. Another day in which she had done nothing, and she could not understand how nothing could leave her so very tired. Her bones ached and her head throbbed, as if she had spent hours behind a plough when in fact she had spent hours wandering these halls, occasionally checking the windows to see if Sara had returned and avoiding the room where her mother rested and read and waited for Rebecca to walk in so she could sit her down and insist that it was time to find another man.

In a way she resented both Hans and herself. She never saw herself as the kind of woman to need a man to make her feel complete. It took Hans dying to reveal to herself exactly how weak she was without the man she had grown with. As a child had she not insisted that men were stupid and pointless, that she could fare far better alone? That insistence had lasted up until the day Hans first smiled at her, and even sometime after that, albeit in a more half-hearted manner. Now he was gone and Rebecca despised the fact that she could not just seem to get up and pick up where she left off. Even the thought of that made her feel sick.

'Rebecca?'

She glanced up. Her mother, Elsa, stood in the doorway, hand steadying herself on the frame, narrowed eyes still sharp even as the rest of her looked about ready to crumble at any second.

'You should be resting,' Rebecca said with no conviction.

'And you should be leaving this house, and instead you rest. It seems neither of us know what is healthy.' Letting go of the door, Elsa hobbled towards the table. Rebecca rose slightly, ready to guide her, but the old woman shooed her away as she lowered herself into her favourite chair.

'It's late, mother,' Rebecca said.

Elsa snorted. 'And when did you start telling me when my bedtime was? I daresay the grave is a long way off for me yet. Until I'm crawling about like a child, I can still do as I please.'

'You may not be crawling like a child but that attitude is reminiscent of one,' Rebecca muttered.

Elsa raised an eyebrow. 'Oh look, a glimmer of humour. I should alert the elders.'

'I wish your illness had robbed you of your humour.'

'Well that's a cruel wish,' Elsa said. 'Humour might be the only reason I'm still here. And don't make some sarcastic comment thanking my humour. It's beneath you.'

'I would say no such thing,' Rebecca said, despite having been about to say exactly such a thing.

'You should count yourself as lucky that I'm still here,' Elsa said.

Rebecca exhaled. That tiredness was going nowhere. She smiled at her mother. 'Of course I do,' she said softly. 'I thank God for it every day. If you had gone as well I...' She shook her head. 'I know you worry about me mother. But you forget I'm a grown woman. When the time is right I will make myself a part of this community again. I promise. But you have to let me make that decision in my own time.'

'Everyone makes their decisions in their own time,' Elsa said. 'But we are not supposed to exist in a lonely vacuum. Sometimes we need family to give us a little push, however much we may hate them for it.' She smiled and rested a hand on Rebecca's face. 'Much as I am loathe to admit it, you are right. I need to sleep. As do you. Goodnight Rebecca.'

Rebecca didn't stand as her mother pushed herself to her feet and shuffled back towards her room. Her inclination was always to help, but Elsa was too strong willed to allow that, and Rebecca feared there was enough strength left in her to administer a swift kick to anyone who tried.

Alone again, she closed her eyes. She thanked God, as she did every night, that her mother had survived her illness, that she still had a daughter, that she still had her own health. Then she reminded herself that that health may not last if she didn't get some sleep. Her mother was right about that, at least.

But she didn't move. She just sat there until the candles were stubs and the first glimmers of morning light came through the window.

She maintained her smile until Sara had run out the door the next morning, on her way to school. She wondered if the other mothers whispered about the fact that she did not accompany her daughter on the way, but the fact was the school was not that far and frankly the prospect of facing either their false cheeriness or unconcealed pity filled her with dread. Part of her wondered if she would punch one of them, part of her if she would break down and cry then and there. And how would they react to either? More pity, or perhaps growing whispers that it had been a year, that it was time for her to move on. If those whispers had not grown already.

She shook that off. Gossip didn't concern her, not really. Not as much as the changed attitudes of all her friends, who at first had visited her every day when all she wanted was to be alone then less and less when she started to need people around her again. And when she did see them, it was always with that slight tightness in their voice, the widening of their eyes on every word that might be hard for her to hear. In the end it became easier to have nothing to do with any of them because the perpetual reminders of her pain weren't doing anything to help it go away. And that avoidance meant that leaving the house became a fraught, difficult experience no longer worth the trouble.

That was not to say she didn't leave occasionally. It was just a matter of timing. Finding the places where nobody would be during the hours when everyone was occupied; whether at work or tending their children or at school. During those times she would head for the stillness of the forest and enjoy herself away from Elsa's prying and the responsibility to be strong for Sara. She could just... be. And after the year she had had, that was a precious thing indeed.

Today, she decided, was a day for that. An hour of fitful sleep had not done much for her weariness, but in the forest at least she could be tired in daylight, surrounded by the beautiful green and smell of nature. And with Sara having disappeared down the path and Elsa still in bed, there was no better time than now.

So she set out, avoiding the path and heading left across the grass. It was a sunny day, the skies were clearer than they had been in a while and she could smell the warm, familiar, distant scent of the harvest. It used to be her favourite time of the year, watching Hans at work, trying to look tough and manly with all the elders, while she giggled like the stupid little girl she had sworn she'd never be.

She shook that thought off. Grief was everywhere all the time. It didn't have to be here at the one time she let herself be away from it.

Nearing the forest, she stopped. Somebody was watching her. She turned, arranging her face to give no sign of joy or sadness, no opportunity for anybody to gossip about what her expression might mean.

Somebody was watching her, somebody she saw immediately. From a distance she immediately recognised the tall, thin figure of Samuel. Always strange, always mysterious, barely ever speaking; as children he had been a fascination, as adults he was a curiosity, at all times he was generally avoided. Samuel's quiet intensity and withdrawn nature led to rumours and nobody liked being associated with rumours.

Rebecca refused to look away. She could barely make out his face at this distance, but she prided herself on not being thrown by anyone. And Samuel had always seemed kind to her, even if now she was somewhat unsettled by him. But nonetheless, she held her ground. She would not be the first to scurry away.

Samuel raised a hand and tipped his hat slightly. Then turned on his heel and was gone, almost as suddenly as he had apparently appeared.

It took Rebecca a moment to realise her heart was beating slightly faster. Had the day grown hotter? She shook her head. Strange as Samuel was, she would not let her tiredness exacerbate that. She had no need to be distracted by Samuel of all people when she had promised this time to herself. She turned and kept walking into the trees.

The entire settlement always seemed peaceful, but compared to everything else the forest was the eye of the storm. There was no sign of human interaction, no sign of anything other than serene nature;

the gently swaying branches, the scrubby bushes, the tweeting birds and occasional scurrying form of a squirrel.

She glanced behind her. She was deep enough now to see only forest in all directions. She smiled and closed her eyes. Here it was easy to pretend that nothing else existed, that this solitude and sanctuary were everything. If there was no-one else in the world, she couldn't lose anyone ever again.

'Rebecca?'

It was as though somebody had dropped a boulder in calm water. Hearing someone else here was wrong, somehow, as absurd as that thought was. The forest, after all, was free to visit for the entire community. She forced away the anger and turned to face the intruder.

Hands in pockets, Erik stood there, smiling below the wide brim of his hat. Tall, handsome and muscular with the perpetual glint of a joke in his eye, Erik was very well loved in the community. Rebecca quite liked him herself, but at that moment she wasn't predisposed to like anybody, especially not someone who had interrupted her walk.

'Yes?' she said.

'I saw you heading into the forest. I thought I'd see if you were alright.'

'Why wouldn't I be?'

Erik shrugged. 'I don't know. I worry. Everyone worries.'

'There is no need to worry about me,' she said.

'Well it's hardly up to those who need worrying about to decide on the need,' Erik said.

'Maybe it should be,' she replied. 'I don't mean to be rude Erik, but I'm in no mood.'

He nodded. 'That's just it Rebecca. You've been in no mood for a year now. Isn't it time you let somebody talk to you again? You never know; that somebody might be able to make you smile.'

'Would the somebody you refer to be yourself by any chance?'

Erik's smile grew slightly. 'What gave it away?'

'I'm happy not smiling,' Rebecca said. 'If that changes, I'll let you know.'

Erik took a step towards her, his expression growing serious. 'Rebecca, we all miss the frustrating, impetuous girl you used to be.'

'That girl could be frustrating and impetuous,' Rebecca snapped. 'That girl didn't have to care for a sickly mother, didn't have a daughter. That girl hadn't lost...'

Dizziness hit for a moment and was gone. Rebecca took a deep breath. Those moments were fewer and fewer, moments when the weight of Hans' death made her lose balance. A year was a long time in many ways, but in too many others it wasn't nearly long enough.

'How long it takes me to get back to myself is my business and mine alone,' she said. 'I may never be who I was again, and I have come to terms with that. It's time everyone else did too.'

'But we wouldn't be your friends if we accepted that,' Erik said. 'I'm here to help, whether you want me to or not.'

'Ah yes, I do love it when my own desires are not taken into account,' Rebecca said.

'Tomorrow night is the dance,' he said. 'I think you should come.'

Rebecca placed her hands on her hips. 'Is that so?'

Erik nodded. 'Consider it a favour to me.'

'What if I don't want to give you a favour?'

'Then let me offer a favour in return,' he said. 'Come to the dance with me, stay at least an hour, and if you don't like it I will leave you alone. Don't come, and I will take it that you still need help coming back to the world.'

'That's not fair,' she said. 'All I want is to be left alone Erik, is that so great a request? Respecting my wishes should be reason enough.'

'Rebecca.' He paused, watching her. 'Rebecca, what life will you have if you remain alone forever? What life will your daughter have without a father? I know you think you can do it all alone and you probably can, but that does not for a second mean that you *should*.

Hans would not want you to spend the rest of your life a lonely widow. You deserve better than that. You deserve happiness and you do not do anyone wrong to allow happiness for yourself. You just have to take the leap.' His smile returned and he tipped his hat. 'I'll be at your house tomorrow evening to see if you want to come to the dance. Please do. Even if there is a very real risk of you enjoying yourself.' With that, he turned and, whistling in a supremely irritating way, headed back out of the forest.

Rebecca watched after him, not moving. Annoying as he was, his words were repeating themselves again and again in his head. *You do not do anyone wrong to allow happiness for yourself.* Was he right? Was she avoiding happiness for fear of dishonouring Hans' memory? The warm day suddenly seemed much colder. It was the kind of thought she preferred to not have to deal with. Perhaps it was true, and perhaps it seemed the right thing to do, but how would she feel looking back in her old age, thinking on all those wasted years? She closed her eyes. Perhaps going to the dance wouldn't be the worst thing. Perhaps.

She took her time heading home. It wasn't a long walk, but she could drag it out if need be, letting herself be distracted by any pretty thing she saw, enjoying the deep breaths of fresh air, staring up into the clear blue sky, wandering along like a daydreaming child. She let any thought enter her mind except those of Erik and the dance. Tomorrow she could think on that. For now, she had gotten away to be thoughtless and she would let herself do exactly that.

Arriving back at her house, she paused on the porch and looked out across the grass, to the distant shapes of the nearest houses, the forest off to the left, the clear blue sky framing it all. She was so very fortunate to live somewhere as beautiful as this, and it would not do to waste that fortune. Life was short and she was surrounded by beauty and good people. Did she have any right not to live when some weren't even given that choice?

It was easier to push that thought away and deal with it later. She opened the door and walked inside. Without Sara here the house seemed still, silent. But her mother should have been up by now. For all her talk of resting, Elsa was rarely tardy. Rebecca frowned.

'Mother?' she called.

No reply. She felt a flicker of concern.

She went straight to the door to her room and pushed it open. Her mother lay on her bed under the blankets, staring up at the roof, blank faced. Something gripped Rebecca's heart and within seconds she was on her knees beside Elsa's bed.

'Mother, wake up,' she said, her heart pounding through the cold vice that had closed around it. 'Mother, please wake up, don't do this, please mother!'

Elsa's chest was rising and falling very slightly. *She was alive.* But why wasn't she replying? Rebecca shook her, gently first then roughly when she didn't rouse or react. Fire and ice were alternating through her veins as images raced through her head, a succession of memories of the moments after Hans' death and flashes of what could be ahead, a life without her mother, another loss to contend with right when she was coming to terms with the first.

Tears in her eyes, breathing ragged, she stumbled back out into the house, bursting through the front door into sunlight that should not still be so warm and pleasant. And she yelled, yelled for someone, anyone, anyone who could come and help. She didn't know how or what they could do and it didn't matter. She just needed somebody.

A shadow fell over her. She looked up. She did not remember falling to her knees. Everything was so blurred and confused.

'What is it?' Samuel asked, no inflection in his voice, no discernible emotion.

'My Mother,' Rebecca managed. Absurdly it occurred to her how much she sounded like a child.

Samuel hurried past her into the house. She forced herself to stand and moments later he had returned, Elsa in his arms as he hurried down the path, past Rebecca. It took her a moment to catch her bearings and hurry after him. She wanted to ask if Elsa would be alright, to ask what he thought, but composure was returning in the face of her need to be calm. Samuel did not know the answers. The doctor would.

They arrived at his small house. Samuel yelled for him and Kai, short, stocky and somewhat round, met them within moments. He directed Samuel to bring Elsa inside and firmly told Rebecca to wait when she tried to follow. Taken aback, she did, only to be joined after a few seconds by Samuel. He met her gaze, they stood like that for a moment, then, without a word, he stepped forward and embraced her.

Was it untoward? Inappropriate? Strange? Yes, but Rebecca did not care. She embraced him back. Comfort was a port in the storm of confusion and fear, and Samuel, at that moment, was the only one offering her comfort. Not the cheap, false comfort of tittered platitudes and whispered enquiries about her wellbeing, but simple, physical presence with no expectation of her saying anything more than she wanted to. He would just be there as long as she needed. Even if she could have spoken, she lacked the words to tell him how grateful she was.

It did not feel like that much time had passed when the door opened and Kai emerged. Rebecca let go of Samuel and turned to face him. He smiled.

'A seizure,' he said. 'Not a serious one. Common, in her condition. I have given her some medication, she will be alright.'

That vice around her heart, familiar from Hans, loosened. She had forgotten it was there. Sometimes you became accustomed to the worst feelings. But that did not matter. Rebecca laughed through renewed tears.

'Thank you doctor,' she said.

'I would like to watch over her a little longer,' Kai said. 'Samuel, take Rebecca home, would you? That was a scare no-one should have.'

Usually Rebecca would have snapped that she could take herself home, but she was too shaken and too grateful to do anything of the sort. So she just nodded, thanked Kai again, and followed Samuel as he began to walk.

In silence they made their way back to her house. The day seemed pleasant again; more than pleasant, beautiful. Relief, Rebecca realised, was the most potent emotion there was, especially when you had been in situations that did not end with it.

'Your mother is a strong woman,' Samuel said finally.

Rebecca nodded. 'Very.'

'It seems that runs in the family.'

She glanced at him, a little confused. 'What do you mean?'

Samuel shrugged. 'You proceed with such dignity, despite losses that would cripple most. But you do not pretend to be happy or ready to move on, despite people's judgements. I think most people going through grief force themselves to smile and move past it so that they can distract themselves, rather than properly dealing with what ails them. You won't distract yourself. You tackle grief head on. I doubt I would have the constitution.'

Rebecca laughed. Relief had the side effect of making you as giddy as a school girl, but she didn't care. 'You? Samuel, you are the toughest person in the community.'

Samuel smiled and Rebecca almost stopped in her tracks. Had she ever seen that before?

'It's funny how fear can be mistaken for many things,' he said. 'No Rebecca, I am not tough at all. Just scared.'

'Scared of what?' she asked, as bemused as she was fascinated.

Samuel paused for a moment. He looked up at the sky, frowning. But if he had wanted to say anything, he gave no sign of it. He kept walking and Rebecca had to hurry to keep up.

They reached the house and came to a halt. Rebecca turned to Samuel, ready to thank him again, but he was already speaking.

'I know Erik wants to convince you to come to the dance,' he said. 'I know he is pressuring you. If you feel you should, then do. But never feel like you must do anything because somebody tells you to. Never.' A ghost of a smile touched his lips, he inclined his head, then with a mumbled good day turned and was on his way again.

Rebecca stared after him. Some strange new feeling had mingled with her relief. Something that was both heavy and light at once, if such a thing were possible. Something that was just making her more confused than ever.

Elsa returned home with Kai later that evening with almost no sign of her ailment. When Sara asked where she had been the old woman made some quip about nosiness being a sin and that she had important business to attend to, which Sara laughed at, leading to a playful argument that had Rebecca smiling as she made dinner.

She had not told her daughter about the day's scare. Rebecca did not want her to fear potentially losing her grandmother as well and besides, Elsa gave no sign of anything being wrong. That old woman would outlive the rest of them.

So the evening progressed normally. The three of them had dinner together and Rebecca said very little, only picking at her food as she looked between her strong, indefatigable mother and her curious, strange daughter. What if today had gone differently? What if only two of them had sat at this dinner table? Rebecca didn't want to think about it, but the image of her mother's blank face staring at the ceiling seemed seared into her memories. That, plus the words of bother Erik and Samuel, meant that she felt well and truly tired and confused by the time she sat down to read Sara's bedtime story.

The tediousness of it seemed more comforting than ever tonight, and by the time the tortoise beat the hare through being slow and steady Rebecca felt more calm than she had all day. She closed the book and looked down at Sara, who was frowning as if deep in thought.

'What is it?' Rebecca asked.

'You didn't sound bored tonight,' Sara said.

Rebecca smiled. Of course she noticed. 'I'm never bored. It's a good story.'

Sara shrugged, but didn't reply.

For a moment, Rebecca considered her child. She felt scared, for some reason. But if anybody knew the right answer, it would be her daughter.

'How would you feel if I married again?' Rebecca asked.

Sara didn't look at her. 'Are you going to marry again?'

Rebecca laughed. 'I would have to have a prospect, which I do not. No, I mean more... if I moved on. Would you feel like I had betrayed your father?'

'Marrying isn't important,' Sara said. 'But moving on is. You'll betray yourself if you don't.' She met her eyes and smiled. 'I miss father every day. You do too. But we are still alive. I don't think there is any point in being alive if all we ever feel is sadness.'

For a moment neither of them spoke as Rebecca considered her words.

'You're clever, Sara,' she said, after a few moments.

'I know, Sara said.

Rebecca kissed her daughter on the head, then bid her goodnight. She put out the candles and walked out through the still kitchen and into her bedroom. She dressed for bed and then lay down, in her bed which had felt far too big for her for so long. It was always as though she was enveloped in more space than she needed here, and perhaps that was why she barely slept anymore.

But tonight, as she lay down and closed her eyes, she drifted off within moments.

She dreamed of Hans, as handsome and happy and full of life as he had been on their wedding day. She dreamed of dancing together with him below a starry sky. There was no-one else in the world, just the two of them, just that feeling of safety, of home and love and joy. But the music slowed and the dance stopped and Hans, with one last smile, kissed her on the cheek then turned and walked away into the night and Rebecca watched him go but did not call after him, just let him keep walking until the dark swallowed him up and she was alone with the stars.

For the first time in a long time she paid close attention to getting dressed, to ensuring that she looked meticulous. Elsa helped her with her hair and when she looked in the mirror she felt like she was that beautiful young woman again whom everyone had despaired of and loved in equal measure. For a moment, it took her breath away. She turned to her mother. Elsa smiled and kissed her on the head without a word and Rebecca *felt* like that little girl again. But she was no little girl. She was a grown woman.

She met Erik at the front door, meeting his smile with her own. He offered his arm and she took it. Together they walked into the evening.

Was she scared? Perhaps. Excited? It was hard to tell. But whatever strange mix of emotions she felt, it was more than the emptiness that had been her lot for too long now, and that was enough. Erik was talking about something and she smiled and nodded and laughed when he made what sounded like jokes, but she wasn't listening. Her mind was on the terrifying yet exhilarating idea that maybe this could be the beginning of something, the beginning of a real return to herself.

It took seeing the church hall for fear to outweigh everything else. The very image of people milling around out the front reminded her starkly of Hans' funeral and involuntarily her hand tightened around Erik's arm.

'It's alright,' he said. 'I'm here.'

Was that comforting? She didn't know. But she didn't relinquish her grip. Together they approached the doors.

The moment she walked through she could feel eyes on her, from all directions. Were they muttering? Was she hearing her name echoed back at her as people tittered and gossiped? She tried to tell herself she didn't care but this spacious hall felt so much more claustrophobic than the safety of her home had in the last year.

She glanced at Erik, but he wasn't paying attention to her. He was smiling around at everyone and she felt a twinge of discomfort. There was precious little excitement left in how she felt about tonight.

'Excuse me,' she muttered, letting go or Erik and heading straight for a table off to the side. She needed a glass of water and jugs had been left out, surrounded by platters of food. She felt hot, like all the eyes on her were burning. Was it in her head, or was everyone staring at her?

With a trembling hand she poured a glass and gulped it back, then another.

'What are you doing?'

She turned. Erik was standing behind her, looking concerned.

'I need a drink.' She tried to keep calm.

'You look upset.'

'I'm not upset.'

'Rebecca, everyone is here. Everyone is looking. You're flustered.'

'Well you're not helping,' she snapped, and pushed past him to be met with a flock of faces that she knew were familiar but none of whom she could name. Women she had grown up with, had been friends with, the very women she dreaded seeing in the months since she lost Hans.

'Rebecca, are you–'

'You seem–'

'It's so good to see you tonight–'

'Are you here with Erik?'

'Has he asked–'

'When he said you were coming I didn't–'

Rebecca closed her eyes and tried to steady her breathing. 'Please, just let me be.'

'Rebecca is alright,' Erik announced, taking her arm again. 'Go and enjoy the dance.'

She felt herself being guided away, then Erik took her arm and she looked up into his eyes.

'Get yourself together,' he hissed.

'I want to go home.'

'You are embarrassing me,' Erik said. 'Really Rebecca, enough is enough. You can't keep acting in this way, demanding everyone's attention, humiliating the people who try–'

'That is enough.'

The voice came from behind them. Rebecca and Erik turned at the same time to see Samuel standing there, face impassive, hands by his sides. But his eyes...

'What do you want?' Erik asked. 'We are talking.'

'She does not seem to be enjoying the conversation,' Samuel replied.

Erik let go of her and took a step towards Samuel. A hush had fallen over the hall. Now Rebecca *knew* everyone was looking. But she only had eyes for Samuel, standing alone and calm.

'Her happiness is none of your business,' Erik said.

'And it is yours?'

Erik looked Samuel up and down with a sneer. 'Go home Samuel. Nobody wants you here.'

'I do,' Rebecca said.

Erik did not even look at her. 'Be quiet Rebecca,' he said. 'This is between–'

It seemed to happen so slowly, and yet it was over in seconds. Samuel stepped forward and at the same moment his fist sent Erik flying.

'I said that's enough.' Samuel said, as Erik hit the floor with a yelp and several cries went up around the hall. Samuel did not seem to care though. He looked at Rebecca.

She smiled.

Together they walked for the door. People parted as if they were dangerous or contagious, their mouths gaping and their eyes wide, but for the first time she didn't care at all.

They emerged into the cool night air. Rebecca started walking back towards her house, and part of her expected Samuel to stop, but he didn't. Together they walked in silence under the starry sky and Rebecca did not stop smiling until they arrived at her front door.

She turned to face Samuel. For a moment they just stood there in the cool night air looking at each other.

'Nobody has any right to tell you who you should be or how you should feel,' he said.

'I know,' she replied.

For a few seconds all that could be heard was the wind in the trees of the distant forest.

'Thank you,' she said.

He nodded.

'Would you like to come in for a cup of tea?' she said.

Samuel didn't speak. He just smiled. Her own smile grew.

The night had gotten warmer.

The End

TAINTED SPRING

NICOLE PORTER

<u>Chapter 1</u>

"I'll kill you Abigail, I swear it!" Collin yelled.

From the kitchen pantry, Abigail and her daughter, Barbara, trembled together. Every few seconds Abigail squeezed her daughter's hand.

They knew better than to make a sound. Being caught by Collin in one of his rages meant being hit. Or worse.

They'd never seen him this angry.

"Where is it Abigail?" he thundered, his black beard trembling with every word.

He smashed a pan to the floor, and started ripping open cupboards in search of his whisky.

Cupboard after cupboard was torn open. Abigail and Barbara exchanged a tear-filled look. They knew it was only a matter of time.

He flung open the pantry door and they screamed, rushing out. Barbara got away, ran to hide in the barn. But Abigail didn't have a chance. She was Collin's intended target, after all.

Grabbing Abigail by the wrists, Collin flung her to the floor.

"I said where is it?"

Abigail spoke to the wood floor, splintered from another one of his rages.

"It's not permitted. It's against the Ordnung."

He grabbed her by the bun, wrenched her head up to his face.

"You think I care? Women don't understand what hard work is really like."

He shoved her back to her hands and knees.

"You're a fool, Abigail. Always have been, always will be."

Grabbing her by the bun, he wrenched her up again.

"Now tell me – where is it?"

Abigail was sobbing so hard that Collin couldn't make out her first answer at all.

He shook her.

"What did you say?"

"I poured it out. It isn't right – the drinking."

Collin threw her back to the floor.

"Dumb woman."

He kicked her.

"Thinking you know better. You have no idea what I'm dealing with. I need it."

He kicked her again. And again. And again.

Abigail gasped out pleas, cries for him to stop, but his foot seemed detached from him, it kicked on and on, as she rolled to and fro like a rag doll. He only stopped when she fell still.

—

Abigail awoke to a cool cloth being pressed to her forehead. It was so dark she couldn't see anything, though she didn't have to. She knew. It was Barbara.

A low moan escaped Abigail's lips, and this time it was Barbara who squeezed her hand.

"It's ok Mom. It's going to be ok."

Abigail fell silent. She didn't have the heart to tell her daughter that she didn't believe her.

"I love you so much," Abigail said, forcing herself up to a sitting position and embracing Barbara, "More than you know."

It was true. Only her love for her daughter had kept her locked in this loveless, abusive relationship.

"It won't happen again," Abigail said, smoothing Barbara's flyaway hair, "I promise."

She meant it. Never again would she try to stop Collin from drinking. Even though whiskey made his rages worse, getting rid of it was more dangerous.

Barbara yawned.

Painstakingly, Abigail rose, each of her limbs groaning protest.

She had to get Barbara to bed. She didn't want her falling asleep in class again. The poor girl had suffered enough as it was.

Taking Barbara's hand, whispering "Time for bed", Abigail brought Barbara to her room. Then, folding the patchwork quilt just under Barbara's chin, Abigail tucked her into bed. She stroked her daughter's hair as she sang the old lullaby she had sung when she was a baby: "Sleep, my baby, sleep!

Your Daddy's tending the sheep.

Your Mommy's taken the cows away.

Won't come home till break of day.

Sleep, my baby, sleep!"

By the end of the first verse, Barbara had nodded off.

Abigail watched her for a minute: the peaceful rising and falling of her chest with every breath. Sometimes she wondered how something so good could have come from her and Collin. She wondered if her daughter would look so peaceful if she knew what her mother was about to do.

As Abigail walked out of the room, she reasoned with herself. She had no choice. It had been weeks since she had been alone with him. And especially after today's incident she needed to see him or she was going to go crazy.

Abigail tiptoed out of the house and didn't resume a normal tread until she was off their property and on his. Even then, every few steps, she looked around, squinting worriedly through the dark.

There was no need to wonder what would happen to her if she were caught. The whole community would shun her. She would never see Barbara again.

As she neared, Barbara saw a light on in the front porch of the house. As if he knew.

Abigail smiled, then shuddered.

Maybe her cries of pain had been so loud that he had heard them all the way over here.

Abigail knocked four times then once, and then again, four times then once. Nothing happened. Abigail peered in the front door window, but all she could see was more darkness.

What if something had happened to him? What if he wasn't coming at all?

But then the door swung open.

"Ike," Abigail whispered as the face she had come to so love brightened upon seeing her.

As soon as she stepped inside into the light, however, his face fell.

"Not again," Ike said, a break in his voice.

Abigail avoided his gaze, as it slid from her bruised arms to her ripped apron. If she caught his eye, she would start sobbing right there.

"It was my fault. I hid the whiskey. I should've known better."

Anger flashed in Ike's eyes. He stepped forward to seize her hands, stopping himself at the last second.

"That's ridiculous, and you know it. Abigail, please, we should go to Jonah. Tell him about how Collin drinks, the way he beats you."

Abigail's said nothing, kept her gaze on the floor. Ike gestured into the sitting room, to the same plaid armchair as usual.

Abigail went over and flopped down on it. When she glanced over at Ike, he was still waiting for an answer.

So, with a sigh, she said: "You know Jonah would never believe us. Collin is his son. All that would happen is that you and I would be excommunicated, and I'd never see Barbara again."

For a minute Ike stayed frozen in place with his face turned away, as if trying to refuse what had been said. But after a minute, he sighed too, and sat down on the armchair next to her.

"You're right, of course." - he sat up straighter and shot her a smile - "Despite the circumstances, I'm glad to see you."

Abigail spoke to her hands; it had been so long, she felt shy to look Ike in the eye.

"Words can't express how happy seeing you has made me."

She cast him a sidelong glance. Seeing the goofy grin her words had brought to his face, she couldn't hold back a smile of her own.

Ike leapt up.

"Almost forgot, I got you something."

He returned with a small knitted flower that he placed in Abigail's palm.

"So I can be with you always."

Abigail raised the little red and yellow thing to her face, inhaled its pine scent, the pine scent that was Ike's, and smiled.

"Thank you."

Ike sat back down, his smile resting on Abigail contentedly.

"I know you don't like me saying it, Abigail, but I know we'll be together. Don't ask me how, I just know."

Abigail looked at him longingly, wishing his smile could become hers, wishing she could still believe him. But it had been nine years now. Nine years of longing looks and no physical contact, of nighttime visits and daytime stolen glances. Nine years of nothing.

Maybe in the beginning she could have believed Ike. After all, he had bought land right beside Collin's, started working within the church to modernize their doctrine – to allow exceptions to the no divorce rule for the case of immoral spouses.

He had remained a steadfast bachelor all the while – much to the surprise of the community – and nothing else had changed either. The minister and the church were set in their ways, while Collin only grew more angry and violent.

Abigail placed her hand beside his on the arm of her armchair, their hands one thin block of plaid apart. She smiled and closed her eyes.

Yes, for all Ike's talk, she knew this was it. Here, now, these would be her happiest moments, stolen seconds with a man who was not hers, but who was good and kind. Who loved her.

It seemed only a second later that Ike said: "Abigail– get up – quick! It's almost light outside."

Abigail jumped up and raced to the door.

"Goodbye Ike!" she said over her shoulder, "I can't thank you enough. For everything."

"Wait!" said Ike, running after her.

At the door, he pressed something in her hand, paused as if to say something more, then opened the door, gesturing for her to go.

"There's no time – Collin could be up any minute. Hurry!"

As she ran down the road, kicking up dust as she went, Abigail looked at what was in her hand.

The knitted flower. She brought it to her nose, inhaled deep and smiled.

Whatever came today, she could handle it. As long as Collin hadn't woken up yet.

By the time she reached her house, the rooster had started crowing. Abigail could hardly breathe she was running so fast. She threw herself through the door and then –

"Abigail?"

Abigail froze.

Chapter 2

It was Collin. His footsteps pounded down the steps – angrily?

"Yes?"

His face looked sad, sorry.

"I'm sorry Abigail. I overreacted last night. There's just some things you don't know, is all."

Abigail kept her gaze on his feet, his scuffed-up shoes that had kicked her last night and would kick her again.

She nodded, played her part in the charade that had been acted out a hundred times before.

Collin strode past her into the kitchen.

"What – no breakfast?"

Abigail glared at his back.

"I'm sorry. I'll get some cornmeal mush started right away," she said and got to work.

She took several ears of field corn out of the pantry, removed the husks, and started cutting. The whup-whup-whup of her knife was a welcome outlet for her anger.

She hated Collin. Would she ever be free of him? If only something would happen to him, if only he were struck by a horse or had some sort of an accident.

Abigail froze, looking at herself in the glint of the knife. No, no that wasn't right. She wouldn't wish that even on Collin. She would only pray that through God's grace he would come to see the error of his ways.

As Abigail moved on to the next ear, after her first three whup-whups, there was a crash, then a shout.

Abigail ran outside to find Collin splayed out on the ground, an upturned wheelbarrow beside him. The wheelbarrow's dirt had fallen on him and he was half-submerged in it.

Abigail ran up to him and kneeled beside him.

"Collin are you ok?"

Collin's mouth was locked into a snarl, his eyes blinking rapidly, looking at something beyond Abigail.

"Collin?" – she shook him – "Collin?"

And then he fell still.

"No," Abigail said, unable to believe what she was seeing.

"No, no, no," she said, shaking Collin, over and over again.

"Mom?" Barbara called from the doorway, then, kneeling beside her: "Mom? Dad?"

Abigail was still locked in motion, tears spilling down her face onto Collin's still open-eyed, snarling one.

"No, no, no," she moaned, "What have I done? What have I-"

And then together, she and Barbara shook him, the man who had left them behind, wronged them beyond belief, the man they still needed now anyway.

When after a minute or ten, Barbara asked: "Mom, what should we do?", the realization struck Abigail like a slap to the face.

Collin was gone. Dead. She had to get help.

"Wait here Barbara," she told the girl, whose pink face was a river of tears.

It didn't take long for Abigail to run to the church, it was the land on the other side of her house after all. As soon as she ran through the church's front doors she knew something was wrong.

Hannah was sitting erect on a chair in the entrance. On seeing Abigail, her thick eyebrows lowered so much they nearly made her eyes disappear altogether.

"Abigail," her cool voice said as she stood up.

The words tumbled out of Abigail: "It's Collin, he fell, he – you have to come Hannah. Is Jonah here?"

Hannah's mouth drew into a thin line, her hands clenched into bony fists.

"What have you done to my son?" she hissed, before sweeping off into the chapel.

She returned a moment later with Jonah, and they all took off for Abigail's house.

In the grass out front, beside the upturned wheelbarrow, Barbara was in the same position as before. Ike's body, on the other hand, to Abigail looked somehow even worse: his eyes were open wider, while his mouth was even more of a distorted snarl, as if raging against what had happened.

Abigail watched with shaking legs as Hannah and Jonah, bent over their son's body, wept. She held Barbara's hand, which was wet from her daughter's tears or her own; she couldn't tell. She squeezed it.

"Barbara," Hannah said after a few minutes, rising to her feet, "Barbara, come with me."

The old woman held out a pale hand, which was also wet with tears.

"Abigail," Jonah said, rising just as Abigail was about to reply, "Come talk with me."

His tone was devoid of all emotion, his blue eyes gray. Hannah, however, was looking at Abigail like she had strangled Collin with her bare hands. Something was going on.

"Abigail," Jonah said softly, and that was when Abigail understood that none of this was a choice.

Abigail nodded, hugged Barbara goodbye and watched as Hannah stalked back towards the church with her daughter's little hand trapped in her bony grip.

"Shall we?" Jonah said, gesturing to the house. They walked in through the kitchen, the remnants from before the accident strangely chilling: the half-cut-up corn, the still-ajar pantry door. Abigail looked down: even her apron was still on. And to think, less than an hour ago, last time she was there, it hadn't happened yet.

Jonah sat on a chair and gestured for Abigail to do the same.

"Hannah saw you last night," Jonah said as soon as she sat down.

Abigail knew then that it was all over.

Still, she tried to get the words out, tried to get her say in, before what Jonah said made his decision final.

"Jonah – please – I swear to you, there has been nothing untoward.. I have always been faithful to Collin, despite..."

She let the sentence trail off, didn't say despite what; Jonah and Hannah had always been blind when it came to their only son.

Jonah didn't even glance at Abigail; he spoke to the cut-up corn, as if it was more worthy of his attention.

"I don't know much about much, but I do know that this doesn't look good, that the Bishop will have to be informed. And now that my son has died..." Jonah gave her a long, hard look – "This doesn't look good at all."

"Jonah, I-"

He held up his hand.

"For the time being, I think we can all agree that it's best that Barbara stay with Hannah and me-"

"Jonah, please-"

He held up his hand again, this time something of Collin's dying snarl on his face.

"I wasn't finished. In the meantime, we will be bringing this to the attention of the community, to see what they have to say. Ike has always been a good parishioner. If he has engaged in anything untoward, Hannah and I have no doubt that it is because he has been seduced into it by you. From the start, you have not behaved as a wife should."

Jonah rose.

"You may find that you will be excommunicated in the next week or so for what you have done. May God forgive you Abigail."

Abigail rose.

"Jonah," she said, "Please..."

But he strode through the door and away, as if he hadn't heard her at all.

Chapter 3

After Jonah had left, Abigail watched the door swing in and out, in and out, stared at it for a while, as if Jonah might come back. As if there was the smallest chance that things would be made right.

Finally Abigail directed her gaze to the chopped-up corn bits, which was what she'd be soon: cut off, alone.

A great tiredness descended upon her, and she made her way upstairs and collapsed into bed.

Abigail awoke crying once, a hundred times. Each time she couldn't bear to get up, and rolled to the other side, lay there until she fell back asleep again.

Finally, when she couldn't lie down for another second, Abigail got up and stumbled out into the hallway. According to the clock, a day had passed, maybe two.

She stumbled out onto the street, hardly knew where she was headed. She couldn't go to Ike, not now, probably not ever. She only realized her destination when a collie scampered across the street.

Mercy. Of course. Her collie was named Abraham. Mercy was all Abigail had left now. They'd been friends since Abigail was a kid, Mercy wouldn't abandon her now.

The further Abigail walked, the less sure she became, however. No one would look at her. First were Noah and Miriam, who crossed to walk on the other side of the street. Further down the road, Patience kept her fiery gaze locked on her feet as she passed.

Abigail used to love this long walk to Mercy's farm, which was situated at the edge of the community's land, seeing all her friends as she walked. Now, she wasn't sure she could make it at all.

Further down, on a house porch, Abigail passed Otto and Roman, their conversation stopping as abruptly as if she'd cut it with scissors herself.

The rest of the way, Abigail kept her gaze on her feet. They were bare, dirty and calloused.

Like most women, she went shoeless in the summer to avoid wearing out her shoes. Her left pinky toe was still bent funny from when Collin had slammed his boot down on her foot.

As soon as Mercy saw Abigail, she walked out to meet her.

"Abigail," she said.

Mercy's face was white and though her lips had spoken Abigail's name, her eyes didn't seem to be seeing her.

"Mercy," Abigail said, stepped forward, for a hug.

Mercy stepped back, looked over her shoulder. Samuel was standing on the porch, watching them.

"I heard what happened," Mercy said.

Abigail shook her head.

"No, Mer, no, none of what they're saying is true. Jonah's death was an accident, I don't know what happened. Sure, he was mean – you knew that, but I didn't do anything to him. I swear it."

Mercy nodded, though her eyes still looked through Abigail.

"And Ike..." Abigail began.

Mercy looked over her shoulder to Samuel again.

"I think you should go, Abigail."

"But Mercy," Abigail said, her eyes searching her friend's face for some uncertainty, some sadness, anything.

But Mercy looked at her like a stranger and turned her back on her and left.

Abigail stood there for a minute, her eyes burning with tears, at the pain of it, at the humiliation. Seth and Sara were passing, staring with that same hard look all of them wore now – as if she had been excommunicated already.

Abigail wiped her eyes and exhaled. Then, she ran.

She wasn't going to give any of them the satisfaction of seeing her cry. She ran without seeing – her vision blinded by tears and the dust her feet were kicking up, without hearing – the rasp of her breath and pounding of her feet louder than anything else.

When she got back to her house, Jonah was waiting in the kitchen, sitting on the same chair he had been in before.

"Abigail," he said, when she walked in, "Sit down."

Abigail shook her head.

"Tell me," she said in a quavering voice, though she already knew, "Tell me Jonah."

"The Bishop has been informed of the situation and is investigating the case. In the meantime, the community has made a decision."

Jonah gestured to the chair again, and, in a voice devoid of feeling, said: "Are you sure you don't want to sit down?"

Abigail shook her head again. It was the only thing she was sure of: that she would not take whatever he had to say sitting down.

"You are to be excommunicated pending the outcome," Jonah said, and Abigail found that the only thing she really did need now, was a chair.

She staggered to the counter, grabbed onto the edge for support.

"Barbara will of course stay with us in the meantime," he said, rising, his task done.

Abigail whirled around.

"No – Jonah – please, please, I'm begging you-"

She seized the edge of his coat. He looked at her, his mouth rising into Collin's same death snarl.

"Goodbye Abigail," he said, wrenching his coat free and striding out the door.

Abigail rushed after him.

"Please Jonah – I have nowhere, nothing – Collin left me nothing you know, nothing – and Barbara, my daughter, my dear sweet daughter – please, I'm begging you."

Jonah stopped, turned to face her.

"The community's decision is final."

Even as he continued on, Abigail staggered after him, her feet slipping and her entire body falling into the same dirt no one had cleaned up since Collin's death.

There, belly-down in the dirt, Abigail raised her head and screamed into the sky.

Then she screamed again and again, until her voice was hoarse and she let her head drop into the dirt. There was nothing to do now, except lay there and die.

—

Abigail awoke shaking. She squinted open her eyes to see blinding sun—then closed them again.

"Abigail are you alright?"

At Ike's voice, Abigail opened her eyes again and accepted the hand that was offered her. She was pulled to a seated position, and Ike sat on the ground across from her.

"I heard what happened."

Abigail looked away, to her house. The front door was still open.

"You shouldn't be here Ike."

"What does it matter now, Abigail? They've excommunicated you unfairly. This is wrong. From the start you've been the victim and now you're being blamed as the criminal."

The front door to her house was swinging softly in the breeze. Abigail shook her head, still unable to bear looking at Ike.

"I've been a bad wife, a bad mother. I've betrayed Collin in my thoughts – and in my actions. And now I'm being punished for it."

Ike seized her hand. Abigail's eyes fluttered to his as she drew back. Never before had they touched each other like that.

"Betrayed? Abigail, if anyone has been the betrayer, it's me. I'm the one who has been pursuing you from the start – at the beginning you were the one who begged me to leave you be – don't you remember? This is my fault, and I'm going to make this right."

Ike stood up, and offered his hand to Abigail. Without taking his hand, Abigail wobbled her way upright.

"You have more faith in the community then they warrant, I'm afraid," she said.

But Ike's head was already turned towards the church, his tanned face hopeful, his blue eyes clear.

When he turned back to Abigail and clasped her hand once more, his mouth was set in a determined line.

"I swear it to you Abigail. I said it once and I'll say it again, we will be together. I will make this right."

Abigail said nothing more, her gaze on her own muddied feet and front. Ike's gaze was still on the church – he couldn't see it. See that she was muddied beyond cleaning.

—

Ike walked Abigail back to her house. He cleaned up the kitchen – finally throwing out those horrible rotting corn kernels, made her some tea. And then he left. As he went, he cast a look around the darkened room, the night casting everything into ominous-looking shadows.

"Mark my words Abigail, this house will be different by the time I come back. Soon, everything will be different."

Abigail nodded, managing a half-hearted smile as he left. She looked at the shadow of the pantry, the door still open. She sure hoped Ike was right. If not, there would be nothing left for her.

—

Abigail waited and waited. She couldn't sleep before she had found out. She couldn't bear waking up with the crushing weight of her excommunication upon her.

But the wait seemed to stretch on forever. Abigail found herself nodding off, and the next thing she knew her front door was opening.

Ike was back, except it was still dark out, and the house was the same.

He said the words Abigail had known he would:

"I'm sorry, Abigail."

And then he said: "It's not hopeless, however, the community said they'd let me address everyone and have another vote on it tomorrow. I know I can convince them Abigail, I'm sure of it."

It was too dark for Abigail to see Ike's face, but the hope of his words got lost in the shadows all around her.

"Abigail?" Ike asked.

"Yes?"

"I spoke to my brother at the church too. He was Collin's closest friend. He hasn't told anyone yet, but Collin had a heart condition. It made Collin stressed all the time, maybe even made him so stressed that he drank."

Abigail nodded, slowly, the revelation hitting her as a blow to the chest. All this time, and Collin never told her. And to think that she had judged her poor sick husband so harshly.

Ike continued: "Philip never told anyone because Collin made him swear not to. He was too proud. Philip still doesn't want to tell anyone, but I know can convince him."

Abigail nodded again, this one only a hollow repetition of the first.

"I should go now," Ike said, "They're going to be watching the two of us closely. I'm sure Hannah and Jonah are eager to discredit me. But there's hope Abigail!"

"Yes," Abigail said.

He clasped her hand again, and, as he left, with the other she squeezed the knitted flower tightly.

It was for the best that Ike didn't know, didn't realize just how doomed the situation was. He had never been there when it was just her and Philip, so he'd never seen the way his brother looked at her, never seen the suspicious hatred in his little eyes.

Now that Abigail was alone she pressed the little flower to her check and broke down sobbing.

—

This time when Abigail woke up it was still dark, but she was moving. Abigail sat up, and was shoved back down.

When she opened her eyes she saw only darkness. She tossed back and forth but was kicked in the back over again and over again until she fell still. Pain still ratcheting down her back, Abigail let out a soundless moan. Her lips quivered under the gag. Her arms and legs were bound.

Her eyes were blindfolded. She was in some sort of bag. All she could do was roll – and not even that, for she would be kicked. No, all Abigail could really do was wait in terror for what was to come.

Chapter 4

While her body lay bound and useless, Abigail's terrors were given free reign. Who was doing this to her? She could hear the clop of hooves so it had to be someone from the community. Hannah? Jonah? Was the whole community in on it? Was God finally doling out the punishment she so justly deserved?

Forgetting herself, Abigail crumpled herself in a ball – and was kicked again – sending a new stream of tears down her cheek.

Where were they taking her? Were they going to throw her in some ditch – leave her there to die? Or worse - throw her in the lake, where her body would probably be rotted to unrecognizability before it was ever found?

Abigail shuddered at the thought.

Then again, would being thrown out of the community be any worse? No, Abigail realized, being thrown out into the outside world would be as good as a death sentence. She couldn't survive out there.

At some point, the horses' hooves fell silent. Then came the sound of footsteps, of unzipping. Abigail was unrolled and untied. Only her blindfold and gag were left on.

"Don't move," said a gruff voice she didn't recognize, "If you move in the next 5 minutes, I'll shoot you."

She was kicked once. Then she heard footsteps, then the clop of horses' hooves. Then silence.

Abigail wondered how she was supposed to be sure that five minutes had passed. She counted to a hundred in her head a few times.

When something landed on her and started cawing, Abigail shook, pulling off the blind and then the gag. A crow flew off, away into the gray sky.

Below the gray sky was more gray: she was in some concrete place. Abigail pinched herself, closed her eyes once more. But there was no escaping it – she was awake.

At her feet were the remains of what she had been tied and transported in: a large black duffel bag and several pieces of rope.

Abigail stared at them for a minute, trembling.

So the community had done it – not only excommunicated Abigail from her home, but actually physically removed her from it. If the way whoever had taken Abigail treated her was any indication, returning wouldn't be safe. Now, Abigail would never see her daughter or Ike again.

Abigail thought back to Rumspringa – the time when she had been a teenager and allowed on trips into the city to explore the outside world. Now, the knowledge she had gained on these trips would be her lifeline.

Abigail began walking towards a road she could see in the distance. Hopefully she could get a car to stop, tell her which way the nearest city or town was.

Now she had nothing– no money, only the muddied and now torn clothes on her back. That and the knowledge that cities in the outside world had places for people who had nothing – she'd heard about them– "shelters" they were called.

If she made it to one of those, maybe she would be alright. At least for now, for the next few days. Any farther ahead she didn't have the energy to think about.

As Abigail walked, she smiled at the gray sky.

As long as it didn't rain, it would be fine like this – perfect even. The sun would make her too hot, the dark too cold. The stretching of her legs felt good. Abigail was still on the verge of tears, but crying wouldn't help anyone – least of all herself.

She took out Ike's flower from her brassiere, where the tiny knitted thing had been hidden, and squeezed as she walked. It was almost as if Ike was there with her.

When the first car passed, Abigail was too much in her own thoughts to notice until it sped right by.

Abigail ran after it, waving, but she was too late.

After that, she stayed on her guard, listened carefully to the sounds of the road. And, when the next car drove near, she was ready.

She turned around to face the coming black Honda and waved wildly, leaning out into the road. She knew the spectacle she have been making with her clothes and gestures, but she didn't care. She had to get a car to stop.

The black Honda, however, zoomed right by, all its occupants on their phones.

Abigail sighed, and continued her trek.

After her first failure, she had three more cards drive by. The latest was the most infuriating, with its young female driver and her male companion gaping at Abigail uselessly.

Finally, after Abigail engaged in her most determined waving bout yet, a silver minivan pulled over, and an Einstein-haired man peered out of a window.

"Please, where is the nearest city?" Abigail asked.

The window descended, and the Einstein-haired man squinted at her.

"Waterloo is four hours or so that way," he said.

He swept his hand down the long expanse of road that, with the tone of his description, seemed to stretch to infinity.

"Thank you," Abigail said.

She turned away with a sigh.

"Would you like a ride?" a female voice asked.

Abigail turned back to see a white-haired woman behind the man, smiling kindly at her. Abigail stared at them for a minute. They looked like good people.

"Ok," she said.

An older boy in the back seat swung open the door, and Abigail got in.

She sat down in the middle seat and soon found herself awash in conversation.

The Salisowells were kind and curious, but not pushy. They took her claim that she was "visiting the city" at face value, regaled her with stories of Waterloo's recent heritage train that took visitors through town.

It was with a sad longing the Abigail took in the couple's clasped hands in the front of the car, their wrinkled fingers entwined. Maybe life could have been different for her, if she hadn't met Collin.

At Abigail's request, they dropped her off at the train station, which was right in the city center and wished her well. She waved goodbye with the question of where the shelter was on her lips. She had gotten to know them too well, was too embarrassed to ask.

As the silver minivan pulled off, Abigail turned her attention to the train station, its platform flocked with passengers who were all staring at her. She had to get to the shelter as fast as she could.

Swallowing her pride, Abigail strode up to the ticket counter inside the station and asked the man where the nearest shelter was.

With a look of obvious distaste at her disheveled appearance, the man said "Corner of Metcalfe and Cumberland."

"Thank you," Abigail said, although the man had only increased her worries. Street names meant nothing to her.

However, as she was walking out, an older woman who had seen their exchange, spoke to her: "You are in search of the Waterloo mission – the shelter? I volunteer there on occasion. I have arrived early for my train. I can bring you to the mission now."

Abigail agreed, and the old woman led her out to the parking lot to a shiny maroon station wagon. Then, the old woman got in the driver's seat, Abigail got in the passenger's, and they were off.

The old woman chattered nonstop to Abigail, who sank into her seat gratefully. It was clear that the woman spoke merely for the act itself and no acknowledgement on the part of her listener was required.

It didn't take long before the maroon station wagon was pulling up to a red-bricked building with a group of scraggly-looking men outside it.

The woman waved to it, saying: "Here we are. Now, just remember what I told you and you'll do fine."

Then, with one final wave, she swept Abigail out of the car and sped away. It all happened so fast that Abigail didn't have time to ask what exactly she had to remember.

Abigail's heart sank as she took in the scraggly-looking men, who were leering at her. Whatever that old woman had told her, it had probably been important.

<u>Chapter 5</u>

Abigail hurried inside the shelter.

At the desk was a severe-looking woman with gigantic silver glasses.

"Yes?" the woman said, throwing a look up at Abigail, then back down at the papers she was writing on.

"I... I would like to stay here," Abigail said timidly.

"Sorry," the woman said, her eyes still on whatever she was writing, "No beds left."

"I don't think you understand," Abigail said slowly, "I have nowhere else to go."

The woman tossed up another look, this one resting on Abigail for a moment, as if she were surprised that she was still there.

"We run out of beds fast. You can come in tomorrow morning and reserve one first thing."

The woman's gaze transferred back to her papers.

"And until then?" Abigail asked.

The woman looked up at her coldly and adjusted her glasses.

Abigail turned and walked out. There was nothing left to do now. No hope left.

"Abigail!"

At the familiar voice, she froze.

That had been, and yet it couldn't be...

"Ike?"

The next thing Abigail knew she was seeing the beaming face of her love and being lifted by his embrace.

Amidst the scraggly-looking men's jeers and whoops, Abigail began laughing and crying herself.

"How did you ever find me?" she asked when Ike put her down.

Ike still spoke with an ear-to-eat grin: "I'd been watching your house, keeping an eye on you. So I saw when you were taken. They were too many of them and they weren't from our community. Hired maybe. Anyway, I followed them, but lost them on the highway. I kept questioning people on the road until I found someone who'd seen you. They told me the nearest town and when I got here, I went to the only place I could think of you going."

Abigail nodded, an ear-to-ear grin stuck on her face too.

Ike seized her hand and squeezed it, "We're going to make a life here, you and I Abigail. It's going to be one crazy life – but we're going to do it- together. We'll build a life here until their decision, and then, regardless, we'll find a way to get Barbara back."

Abigail squeezed his hand back, and looked to the sky. The sun was peeking out between the clouds.

I WOULD LIKE MY HEART BACK NOW

137

MONICA MANN

<u>December</u>

The service had been lovely as always but Hannah had been unable to concentrate, her mind bustling with dozens of thoughts. As she followed her fiancé's family from the home of one of the member and into the back area of their farm, she wrung her hands nervously.

"Hannah, are you unwell?" She jumped at the sound of Isaac's voice near her ear.

"Not at all! On the contrary, in fact," she replied, peering at him, confusion coloring her face. "What would make you ask such a thing?"

"You seemed not to be paying any attention whatsoever during the sermon. I believe the Bishop scowled at you at one moment." Shocked, Hannah paused in mid step to stare at her husband-to-be, abruptly holding up the line trekking through the field.

"You must be joking!" she cried and then saw the twinkle in Isaac's gentle hazel eyes.

"Perhaps I am but you must admit that your mind has been elsewhere today. What are you thinking about? I noticed the faraway look in your eye from my side of the room!" Hannah laughed and continued toward the barn where the Fisher family had arranged for lunch following their Sunday worship. The winter had been unseasonably warm and Hannah felt somewhat overdressed in her wool cloak. She wished for snow. It did not feel festive without snowflakes gracing the air.

"Well? What is it that plagues your thoughts? Are you reconsidering our marriage?" Again, Isaac's warm eyes lit up with laughter and Hannah grinned broadly at his jesting.

"Certainly not! I am simply concerned about Christmas," Hannah replied, her thoughts beginning to race once more. It was Isaac's turn to show confusion.

"What of Christmas? It is the loveliest time of year. Surely you can't be glum!"

"Not in the least," Hannah replied as they made their way into the spacious structure to join the rest of the congregation. "I am simply worried I have not prepared properly. I have made presents of all of the children and for my parents but I feel as though I have forgotten someone. Which brings me to the Christmas cards. I am always concerned that I have left out a family. Can you imagine how much embarrassment that would bring to us should I omit a single family? What's more is I set up the nativity scene in the front of our home and I cannot find one wise man and two angels. Now I suspect that Rachel has been playing with them but I have yet to find them and she denies knowing their whereabouts. I must have father whittle some for me or else it will be a disaster!"

Suddenly Hannah felt as though a huge weight had been lifted off her shoulders with the confession. Isaac burst into laughter.

"Oh, Hannah! The things which make you fret do amuse me endlessly. It is Christmastime, *liebchen*. It is not a time of worry and fret. That is for the English. We are only to give thanks and spend time with those dearest to us."

"I know, Isaac, but I cannot help wanting Christmas to be perfect! It is my favorite time of the year. And look! This year we haven't even any snow! It hardly seems proper to even set up a tree without the candlelight twinkling off the snow." Hannah pouted but immediately smiled as the truth of his words struck her. Of course he was right; this was not a time of stress. Their way was that of peace and order, not to be overshadowed by the trivialities which the outside word concerned themselves. It was what made the Amish community so special; the ability to block out the unnecessary and focus on the beauty of the basics in life. Hannah could not be happier. She and Isaac had become betrothed in February and their impending marriage was announced to the community in October as per tradition. They had plans to wed the following winter as per tradition and she could not have hoped for a better mate. Despite their engagement, Isaac continued to act as though they were newly enamored with one another, bequeathing her with beautiful flowers and penning poetry for her, words which made her warm to her soul. She was excited to begin her life with him. It seemed that the wedding was millennia away, not merely a year.

"Ah, Hannah, you may worry but your Christmas spirit is infectious," Bishop Philips told her, overhearing the last of their conversation. Blushing scarlet, Hannah turned to acknowledge him, bowing her head.

"Your sermon was well received today, Bishop," Hannah told him, trying to recover from her embarrassment. "It is a rare treat to hear you speak lately. I'm afraid we miss hearing your voice in service. I am pleasantly surprised you have joined us today."

"Unfortunately, I have had business in other districts as of late but I am happy to be back at home. I haven't had the opportunity to congratulate on your betrothal. Isaac, you have done well for yourself. The Yoder family is well respected in our district. Perhaps you will bless them with a son." The Bishop smiled at the couple.

"Not that the Yoder women are any less hard working than any of the men in our community. How is your family? I do not see your father here today," the Bishop continued, looking about, a sudden cloud covering his brown eyes. Hannah and Isaac followed his gaze. Hannah's mother, Ruth stood speaking with several other women while her sisters, Rachel and Miriam ran through the barn, playing a game of tag with some of the other children. As the three continued to look about, Hannah felt a stab of panic in her stomach. It was unheard of for her father, Mark to be absent from church services. She had spent the previous week in Isaac's district at a family member's home. Hannah had been slowly learning the workings of his father's farm at the insistence of Mark who thought it best she understood the complexities of her husband's land as much as possible. As Hannah's cousins resided in close proximity to Isaac's farm, the transition had been seamless and it allowed for their sweet courtship to continue uninterrupted. This also meant, however, that Hannah was not as informed as to the comings and goings of her own family. Brow furrowed, Hannah excused herself and hurried over to her mother, despite Isaac's reactionary hand on her arm to stop her.

"*Mamm*, where is *Daed*?" she whispered in her mother's ear urgently without preamble. Ruth gave Hannah a reproving look and politely exited the conversation in which she was involved.

"Mind your manners, Hannah!" Ruth Yoder chided her daughter.

"I'm sorry Mammi, I am just worried about him. It is unlike him to miss service. I can't recall one instance prior to this one in fact!" Hannah insisted. Seeing her oldest daughter's distress, Ruth's face softened.

"Your father was away at market in Pittsburgh over the weekend. He was expecting to be back last night but the weather turned so he must have been detained. He will likely be home when we return." Hannah exhaled with relief and returned to her fiancé and the Bishop where she reiterated what she had been told. A bell rang to indicate that the meal was about to be served and they all sat at the long tables set up in the middle of building. Yet as they bowed their heads and grace was said, once again, Hannah felt herself distracted by unstoppable thoughts. This time, however, they were not of snowfalls and wise men. Suddenly she her mind was focussed completely on the whereabouts of her father.

"I don't mind, Hannah but I cannot help but feel you are overreacting somewhat," Isaac informed her as they pulled their carriage toward the Yoder farm.

"He is my father. I must know that he is well, Isaac," Hannah replied.

"*Liebchen*, he has been going to market since well before you were born. I am sure he is well. You will see." Isaac smiled boyishly at her and encouraged the horses onward. Hannah felt an uncharacteristic smidgen of annoyance at his placation. She gave him a sidelong look but said nothing. She hoped he was right but some inherent sense told her something was amiss. Inclement weather or not, Mark Yoder would have been at worship. His devotion to God was his priority, probably above his own health and safety. Hannah knew her father. He would have risked riding in a blizzard to honor his commitment to the community. Her mother had arrived back from the Miller farm with Rachel and Miriam and the pale afternoon light was already becoming dark, forsaking dusk altogether.

"I do not see his wagon," Hannah mumbled as they pulled to a stop. Alarm growing in her chest, Hannah recognized the Bishop's carriage which was parked behind the modest house. Hannah did not wait for Isaac to escort her from her seat and instead was running up the front steps to toward the door. As she flew inside the house, she stopped in her tracks. Her mother was on her knees, surrounded by Rachel and Miriam, a look of shock upon their faces. Tears had slipped from their cheeks to the wood floor. Bishop Phillips stood, solemn faced at the base of the stairs, his hat in his hands, his lips pursed into a fine line. They did not need to speak. Hannah already knew.

January

"Hannah, Isaac came calling again," Miriam told her, pushing open the door to the bedroom where her sister sat brushing her long hair, placing it into sections for braiding. Hannah did not respond. Instead she continued to count the strokes, slowly, meticulously smoothing down the strands.

"Hannah? Hannah!" Miriam strode into the room and snatched the utensil from her sister's grip. The older girl looked up in surprise and instinctively grabbed it back.

"What is it?" she demanded, rising to her feet menacingly.

"Isaac was here," Miriam said again. "He would like you to contact him when you are well."

"I am well, thank you. I am simply busy. With *Daed* in the hospital, fighting for his life, someone needs to help *Mamm* run the farm,

Miriam. I cannot up and run off to help him when Isaac has able bodied brothers there. What does he want from me?" Her words were like a torrent of venom and twelve-year-old Miriam stepped back, shocked at her tone.

"I believe that he wants to know if you're well, Hannah. I don't think he wants you to help him on the farm," she offered, timidly, tears filling her eyes. Hannah was immediately contrite but her anger would not lessen.

"Thank you, Miriam. I will be in contact with Isaac shortly." Her sister immediately retreated from the bedroom, closing the door in her wake but Hannah heard her sister's stifled sob before she retreated down the stairs. Hannah knew that her tone had been unreasonably harsh but she could not seem to alleviate the insurmountable rage which had filled her since the horrendous accident her father had endured a mere month before. The driver who had injured Mark so severely on that lone road heading home from the city had yet to be caught and Hannah knew she would not rest until the person had been apprehended and brought to justice. Christmas had come and gone in an unmemorable blur, still filled with family and friends but in a much more somber tone than the joy of the season typically brought. The family had left the candles lit in the windows well after other members of the community had extinguished theirs, a constant flame for others to keep Mark in their prayers. Hannah remembered thinking that the nativity scene was ruined and she had reprimanded Rachel harshly for playing with the wooden characters, reducing the child to a blubbering mess. Much more than that, Hannah could not recall about holiday. There had been an exchange of gifts but Mark's had lay unopened at the hearth and Hannah did not have any recollection of what she had received. Hannah's mother had continued her duty, tending to the farm and caring for the children and Hannah had stepped in to assist as opposed to joining Isaac. At first, Isaac had attempted to stay nearby, offering his unselfish aide to the Yoder family but eventually

Hannah's increasingly sullen behavior had driven him home to his family's land. Still, he had frequently visited his beloved to see how she was faring. More often than not, Hannah made herself unavailable for reasons no one could comprehend. While she never admitted it to anyone, she blamed Isaac also for her father's fate. *If only he had been more vigilante, heeded my words more carefully when I suggested that something was amiss with father,* she told herself time and again. It did not matter that Mark Yoder had been hit on the Saturday night, well before Hannah had any inkling that there was trouble. In Hannah's grief she was beyond reason and all she had remaining was her intense anger. It was irrelevant whom was the recipient of her rage. It needed to be released and Hannah ensured that it was so. Mark's initial prognosis had been grim. The internal damage to his organs was severe and he had several broken bones. He was still on a life support machine in the hospital where he had been taken following being struck. Hannah could not bear to see her strong, vital father in such a condition and had refused to attend his side despite her mother's pleading.

"Hannah, your father needs you there," Ruth had begged her daughter. "Please swallow your repulsion and spend some time at his side. He can hear your prayers."

"He can hear my prayers from here, Mamm. It makes not difference if I am here or there. I cannot bear to see him in such a state with wires poking out of him. Hospitals are filled with harsh lights and harsher people," Hannah countered. "I will not be any good to him there. He knows I am with him in spirit."

Any amount of argument had been futile and eventually Ruth gave up, attending the county hospital with only her two youngest.

"God will not allow him to be taken from us," Ruth assured Hannah one night, attempting to connect with her distraught oldest child.

"God should not have allowed him to have been struck in the first place!" Hannah had yelled back. "God should have been watching out for him. God should have rendered the driver comatose and on life support!"

There was no point in debating the issue. In her mind, Hannah would not rest until she saw the face of the person responsible for the atrocity writhing in shame, guilt and agony.

February

"Ma'am I understand your anger but there we are doing everything we can."

Hannah's blue eyes flashed but she checked her temper.

"Sir, it has been almost three months and you have absolutely no leads regarding the driver of the vehicle which struck my father. Surely you should be exploring other avenues to catch this animal! Doesn't it concern you that this kind of person is driving on your streets where your children walk?"

"Hannah!" Isaac gently placed his hand on her shoulder as she rose from her chair to confront the police detective at the desk. He turned apologetically to the detective.

"Hannah has been under a lot of stress since the accident," Isaac told the man who nodded understandingly.

"Of course, we fully get that and we sympathize," Detective Adams replied. "I have heard that your father is no longer on life support. We are all very happy to hear that."

Hannah felt her hands clench into fists, her nails digging into her palms.

"Yes, praise the Lord for small favors," she answered shortly, her eyes narrowing, ignoring Isaac's fingers which were now increasing pressure on her shoulder. "However, that does not change anything. Is this why nothing has been done to find the monster responsible? Because he is alive? Next time he may not be so lucky if this person is still on the road!"

"Miss Yoder, I assure you that we are doing everything we can but it is very difficult with the circumstances. There were no witnesses, it was a dark road..."

Hannah threw up her hands. She understood. Mark Yoder was not a priority to these people. He would have to be dead or English for them to care. They were just going to say words until she left them alone. Worried she would not be able to contain a barrage of words threatening to escape her lips, she turned to leave without responding. Hannah heard Isaac apologizing for her rudeness once more but Hannah did not wait for her fiancé. Moments later, he was at her side, breathing heavily from chasing her down the crowded street. Under normal circumstances, Hannah would have been unnerved by the throng of people in her midst. It was not like her to visit town, much preferring the quiet way of her community but it had been months and there had been no advancement regarding the driver who had struck her father. Against her mother's pleas, Hannah had taken it upon herself to meet with the detective face-to-face.

"Please, Hannah, Bishop Phillips has been in constant contact with the police. You must not go and bother them."

"If not me, then who?" Hannah had demanded.

"Go see your father! He needs you!" Ruth implored. But the words had fallen upon deaf ears and Ruth had summoned Isaac to accompany her now wayward daughter into town. Isaac had appeared as Hannah was setting off.

"Hannah! That was rude!" He breathed, struggling to keep up with her brisk stride.

"Well perhaps that's what they need, rudeness. Niceties don't seem to be getting us anywhere."

"Hannah, I'm sure they are doing everything they can – "

"It is not enough!" Hannah snapped. Isaac stopped walking, taken aback by her tone. Hannah had never had occasion to speak to him in such a manner. He watched after the woman he was destined to marry and he wondered what had happened to the gentle, even tempered girl he had courted. He understood she was frazzled, not acting rationally but deep down, he hoped that girl was not lost forever.

<u>March</u>

"Hannah, you have not been at worship in several weeks."

The statement was blunt but not filled with accusation. Bishop Phillips simply stared at her, his brown eyes wise with understanding. She shrugged nonchalantly and did not turn from the hens from which she was collecting eggs.

"God knows where I am," she responded flippantly. Bishop Phillips drew closer to her inside the coop, ignoring the squawking of the animals in his midst.

"It is not simply of God knowing where to find you," he told her, gently. "Worship is a place of community, a place where others can shoulder your burden while asking for the Lord's help."

Hannah reeled around to glare at him.

"What does the community know of shouldering my burden?" she asked. "Can they find the animal who ran down my father like a rabid dog in the street? Have they made him pay penance for the harm he has caused my family?"

A warm, fatherly hand reached her shoulder and the Bishop smiled weakly.

"Perhaps not, child, but your suffering is our suffering also. We grow together and we will support one another. That is what makes us strong. You cannot fight this burden alone."

"I am not alone," Hannah retorted. "I have my family. I have Isaac."

But even as she said the words, Hannah tried to remember the last time she had spent more than a few moments with her betrothed. She could not. She shoved the thought from her mind. It did not matter. The only importance was figuring out who had hurt her father. Isaac would have to understand that her priority was with her father.

<u>April</u>

"Hannah! Hannah!"

Miriam and Rachel's footsteps could be heard reverberating through her bedroom well before the door flew open and the twins appeared. Her heart in her throat, Hannah turned away from the window out of which she had been staring for well over an hour, lost in thought.

"What is it? Is it *Daed*? Is he dead?"

Shocked, the girls recoiled at her words, smiles fading from their lips.

"No!" Rachel cried. "Of course not! Why would you say such a thing?"

In truth, Hannah had been waiting for news of the like and had been since the day he had been hospitalized. Her heart began to slow and she forced herself to smile at her sisters.

"I'm sorry. What is it?"

"He's awake! *Daed* is awake!"

Hannah's slowing pulse picked up speed once more. She flung herself into her siblings' arms and the three rejoiced at the news.

"He is? When did this happen? What did the doctors say?" Hannah whipped the questions at them rapid fire. Ruth appeared in the doorway. Her face was gaunt from exhaustion and emotion.

"He will still need some time to recover in the hospital," Ruth answered. "But his ribs are healing as well as his kidneys." Hannah pulled away from the twins and looked at her mother, her face alight with excitement. *Now we will catch you! Daed will identify the driver and it will all be over!*

"Did he say anything?" she pressed. "Can he identify the driver? Or the vehicle? Does he know who hit him?"

Ruth's sky colored eyes clouded over and she regarded her daughter for a moment.

"Hannah, it is not healthy for you to focus so direly on the driver. God will sort out what to do with him. You must instead think of your father and concentrate on good thoughts." Hannah scowled at her mother.

"I am focussed on *Daed*! That is why I want to find out who did this to him! Why am I met with resistance at every turn? You, Isaac, Bishop Phillips. Am I the only one who cares about seeing justice served?"

Ruth pursed her lips together and did not reply. Hannah continued to stare at her mother.

"Well? What did he say? Did he identify the man or not?" she demanded. Ruth sighed heavily.

"No, Hannah. He cannot speak. He had a stroke."

<u>May</u>

Springtime held the promise of new birth for everyone in the community but Hannah. She found herself tending to chores indoor more and more. Isaac had ceased visiting altogether and Hannah found herself in the police station once a week, hounding Detective Adams mercilessly. Where the women in the community would have typically begun to make suggestions for her wedding, offering assistance and chattering cheerfully of their own nuptials, Hannah found herself almost isolated, something she was quite content in discovering. The feeling of helplessness which had overwhelmed her was becoming a suffocating blanket as more time passed and left her no closer to finding the heathen who had hurt her father. She still had not gone to the hospital to see Mark, despite reports from her family that he was faring quite well. He still had not managed to recoup his motor skills and Hannah did not want the face of a crippled man plaguing her already dark thoughts. She would not rest until someone had paid.

<u>June</u>

"You are attending service."

Her voice was flat and left no room for argument. Hannah opened her mouth to speak but caught the anger in her mother's usually gentle eyes and thought better of voicing her thoughts. Grudgingly, she retreated to her room to ready herself for worship.

The family hosting church services was a neighbor and the Yoder family arrived just as Bishop Phillips rose to speak. He fixated his eyes upon Hannah and began to preach of forgiveness. Hannah closed her ears and averted her eyes. *I will forgive when the driver asks for forgiveness. Not one moment before. And even then, I may not.*

July

He came home on a Tuesday and several members of the community were present to welcome Mark. They brought flowers and honey and bombarded him and the family with well wishes. Isaac and his family had driven in also but Hannah only watched the event from her bedroom window, unable to watch her enfeebled father slowly stumble his way up the steps of the veranda. Her eyes filled with tears but whether they were of guilt or pain, she was not sure. As Mark made his way inside with the help of his wife and two youngest daughters, Isaac lifted his eyes toward Hannah's bedroom window. His own eyes were filled with sadness and Hannah quickly ducked back behind the curtains, not willing to look at him. It had been a long while since they had spent time together and she admitted that she missed his company dearly. She often wondered what he was doing and if he thought of her. The look on his face told Hannah that he did long for her as she did him. Swallowing the urge to run downstairs and beg him for forgiveness, Hannah sat on the edge of the bed. She wondered if anything would ever be the same again.

August

"Hannah! Hannah!"

Rachel almost knocked Hannah over as she barreled into the barn. Hannah looked up at her quickly.

"What is it?"

"*Daed* said his first clear word!" Hannah felt hope swell in her chest.

"What did he say?" she asked, wiping her hands on her apron and following Rachel out of the building, toward the house.

"He said 'Hannah.' He's asking for you!"

September

Progress was swift from that moment onward. Every day, Mark Yoder began to say more. He was required to see a specialist in town to assist him in his walking but Hannah was beginning to see signs of the same, strapping man she had admired her whole life. She found it less painful to be in his presence but she still could not help but feel enraged at his condition. When Hannah did stay at his side, she pressed him for details of the accident. To her relief, he recalled a great deal and Hannah feverishly wrote down the details as Mark remembered, every day adding more to the description. Finally, after three weeks, she had a proper sketch of the vehicle and possibly the driver which she immediately took to the police station. *Now we've got you!* She thought smugly.

October

"Are we still to marry?"

The question startled Hannah as she had not heard Isaac at her back. He had been watching her from the porch as she hummed to herself, picking wildflowers. Oddly, the upcoming wedding had been fresh in her mind for the first time in months. Since delivering the description to the police, Hannah had felt as though they were nearing absolution and a giant weight seemed to have been lifted from her shoulders. She stared in surprise at her fiancé.

"I certainly hope so, Isaac. Are you reconsidering?" She felt faint as she waited for him to answer. Slowly, Isaac made his way down the steps and toward his betrothed.

"I feel as though we have become very distant these past months, Hannah. I wondered if you still wished for us to marry." She met the distance between them and offered him her hands.

"Forgive me, Isaac! I have been consumed with worry for my father. Of course I have never thought for a moment that you and I would not be wed." Isaac eagerly accepted her hands and squeezed them gently, smiling with relief.

"I am glad you have finally decided to forgive and move on," he told her. "I knew the sensible woman I know was in there somewhere."

Hannah beamed back at him.

"It will be very easy to move on once this man is caught! I believe the police will finally catch him now!"

The smile died on Isaac's lips as he stared at Hannah. He realized that she was still consumed with the idea of catching the driver. Wisely, he said nothing but a sense of unease filled his stomach. Would this never end?

<u>November</u>

"You must be very excited with the upcoming wedding, Hannah. It has been quite a year for you and your family. It will be a relief to have cause for celebration over bad times, I would say," Bishop Phillips said after service. Hannah smiled widely and nodded, glancing at Isaac. He smiled meekly.

"Yes, we are looking forward to it. A Christmas wedding may seem a bit ostentatious but it is my favorite time of year and Isaac has been kind enough to indulge my whimsy on this matter," Hannah answered happily.

"Well I think it is a wonderful idea. It will only solidify your union with Christ. I am happy to see your father up and about."

"Yes, he is already back into manning the farm as he was prior to the accident."

"Well that is wonderful news, Hannah. It must certainly alleviate your desire to see the perpetrator arrested. It was not good for you to be so fixated on such negative thoughts for so long," the Bishop told her, turning to nod at other members of the congregation.

"No, Bishop, I can focus on other things now. The police are closing in on the animal now that my father has given them somewhere to look. We will have our justice in due time. I must leave it in their hands now." The Bishop looked at Hannah sharply.

"Your father knows who hit him?"

"He gave a very accurate description of the man, yes," Hannah replied. "But as you say, Bishop, it is in God's hands now. I have decided to focus more on my husband-to-be and deal with the criminal when he is found."

Bishop Phillips nodded, his eyes dark.

"Yes, it is in God's hands," he agreed.

December

The police were standing on her porch and Hannah felt her heart leap into her throat.

"Miss Yoder? Is your father home?" the detective asked her, peering over her shoulder. She nodded eagerly and granted them entry. Mark sat in a rocking chair in the front room. He rose to his feet with an agility he did not possess even two weeks prior.

"Please do come in, officers," he told them, cordially. Awkwardly, the detectives ventured into the humble home and stood in the doorway.

"Have you found the man responsible?" Hannah demanded. "Is that why you're here?"

Mark gave her a reproachful look.

"Hannah, where are your manners? Would you like a beverage?" Both men shook their heads and fidgeted nervously.

"Well?" Hannah demanded when there was silence. "Have you news?"

"Hannah!" Mark chided again but the lead detective held up his hand and nodded.

"Yes, Miss Yoder. We have your man. Someone has turned himself in."

Hannah's face went through a variety of changes; hope, shock and then anger.

"He turned himself in?" she almost yelled. "After one year? What kind of monster lets a family suffer for an entire year before confessing his crime?"

"Hannah..."

"Yes, Miss Yoder but frankly, in these situations, it is extremely difficult to find hit and run drivers. We are very lucky that someone did come forward at all," the policeman interjected. "But I do understand your frustration."

"I doubt it," Hannah mumbled. "Where is he?"

"He is in the county lock up. We would like your father to come with us to see if he can be identified in a line up but he had fully confessed to the accident."

"Who is he? A young, drunk English boy?" Hannah asked contemptuously, already envisioning the short haired punk, smoking a marijuana cigarette. Again, an uncomfortable silence ensued. Hannah stared at the men expectantly.

"Who is he?"

Detective Adams cleared his throat.

"It is someone you know," he said evasively. Hannah exchanged concerned looks with her father.

"Who?" she pressed.

"He is your Bishop. Daniel Phillips."

"Hello Hannah."

Hannah felt her legs turn to jelly as she stared at her much-loved Bishop behind the bars of the county jail.

"It is true," she whispered. "How did this happen?"

"I wish I could explain it to you, child but there is nothing I can say which will take away what you and your family have endured over this year."

"Please tell me what happened," she begged, her eyes filled with tears. The Bishop took a breath and told her the story he had relived in his head over and over since the day it had happened.

He had travelled the road hundreds, if not thousands of times before but Bishop Phillips had not slept more than two hours a night in over three weeks. There had been minor unrest in two of the neighboring districts, some petty squabbling which should have resolved itself but somehow a miniscule issue had become a weeks long debate. He was grateful that he was finally able to return home to his district. The car in which he rode had been a gift from a Bishop in one of the districts who had taken pity upon his constant state of commute. Bishop Phillips had to admit that it was more luxurious than his hard riding horse and cart but he also knew that he should not get too attached.

As the headlights lit the way around the road, his heart leapt into his throat. A doe stood frozen in the road, shocked by the onset. In his exhaustion, it took a few seconds for his reaction time to match up with his vision. He slammed on the brakes and veered to the left of the road, barely grazing the tail of the animal but full on impacting something else; a horse drawn cart. The mare whinnied in pain and shock as the Bishop struggled to steady the still moving vehicle. As all was still, Bishop Phillips opened the door to the car and ran toward the now toppled buggy. Inside lay the still body of Mark Yoder, seemingly lifeless. Bishop Phillips stood stock still, unsure of what to do. I must stay and wait for help, he told himself. Then he remembered the two glasses of wine he had consumed with supper. Slowly, he backed up and slipped back into the car, driving away undetected into the black night.

Tears fell from her lids onto her cheeks as she looked at the broken man before her. She thought of how badly she had wanted him to suffer but all she could think of was how much he had already suffered. He must have wanted to ease her agony a thousand times but had been trapped in his own nightmare.

"I understand that you must loathe me, Hannah. You have every right to feel as such," Bishop Phillips told her, his voice cracking. Gently, Hannah reached between the bars and offered the Bishop her hands. He grabbed them instantly and looked at her pleadingly.

"I forgive you," she said simply.

Christmas

"Oh, Hannah you look beautiful," Ruth told her daughter, embracing her warmly. "I have been looking forward to this for so long!"

Hannah laughed.

"Yes, me too Mammi," she joked and lovingly returned her mother's caress. She looked at herself in the mirror one last time. She vowed to her reflection that with this new start she would forsake all anger and rely on God to give her strength in the worst of times. She knew how fortunate she was that Isaac had been strong enough to stand by her during such a trying time and she would never forget it. She turned and looked at her mother and sisters.

"Are you ready?" Miriam asked, hopping back and forth from one foot to another. Hannah looked around and suddenly her stomach dropped.

"Where is *Daed*?" she asked, feeling a familiar sense of panic seize her. The curtain was quickly drawn and Mark strolled in, his gait strong and perfect.

"I am here, *liebchen*. Do you think I would miss giving away my oldest daughter?" he answered. His voice was slightly slower than it had been but his words were perfectly pronounced. There was no sign of the stroke he had suffered. Hannah exhaled. Everything was right again.